T0160143

THE BOOK OF SHANGHAI

First published in Great Britain in 2020 by Comma Press.
commapress.co.uk

'State of Trance' was first published in *Fiction World* (Xiaoshuo Jie), 2018. 'Woman Dancing under Stars' was first published in *Zhong Shan*, 2010. 'Ah Fang's Lamp' was first published in *People's Daily Overseas Edition* (Renmin Ribao: Haiwai Ban), 2018. 'Snow' was first published in *Shanghai Literature* (Shanghai Wenxue), 2010. 'The Novelist in the Attic' was first published in *The Ones in Remembrance* by Shen Dacheng (Shanghai: Shanghai Literature and Art Publishing House), 2017. 'Bengal Tiger' was first published in *People's Literature* (Renmin Wenxue), 2001. 'Transparency' was first published in *Shanghai Literature* (Shanghai Wenxue), 2019. 'The Lost' was first published in *October* (Shiyue), 2012. 'Suzhou River' was first published in *The Lover's Head* by Cai Jun (Beijing: China Film Press), 2003. 'The Story of Ah-Ming' was first published in *One*, 2016, then published in *All Corners of the Lanes* (Jiedao Jianghu) by Wang Zhanhei (Beijing: Beijing October Literature and Arts Publishing House), 2018.

A CIP catalogue record of this book is available from the British Library.
ISBN: 1912697270
ISBN-13: 978-1-91269-727-4

Supported by the Confucius Institute at The University of Manchester.

The publisher gratefully acknowledges assistance from Arts Council England.

THE BOOK OF SHANGHAI

EDITED BY JIN LI & DAI CONGRONG

Series Editor
KAREN WANG

Contents

CONTENTS

Introduction

SHANGHAI WAS OPENED TO the world as a commercial port after the end of the First Opium War in 1843. As a result of the war, British, American and French 'concessions' (or enclaves) were set up successively in 1845-46. Despite the shadow cast by the humiliating surrender of China's sovereignty over these districts, the colonists residing in them introduced many opportunities for the rest of the city, opportunities that saw Shanghai grow from a small town at the mouth of the Yangtze River to the largest metropolis in the so-called 'Far East'. The influences of a recently industrialised West mingled, interacted and cross-pollinated with the traditions of a culture that had developed over many centuries. As a contact point between East and West, with its unique location, Shanghai paved the way, acting as a testing site where various ideological and cultural ideas were welcomed, accommodated and re-imagined. Among these ingredients was a complex and diverse literary tradition that established Shanghai as, arguably, the literary capital of China.

Shi Zhecun, a short story writer, editor, and key figure in Shanghai's literary scene in the 1930s, once wrote:

> This so-called modern life comes with a variety of
> unique features: harbours heaving with enormous
> ships bustling to and fro, factories reverberating with
> cacophonous sounds, mines burrowing deep
> underground, ballrooms bouncing to the sounds of
> jazz, department stores climbing up and up into
> skyscrapers, wars fought in the air by planes, racetracks
> taking up acres of space... Even the countryside is
> different now to what previous generations must have
> enjoyed. Can the emotions stimulated by this life in
> the hearts of our poets be the same as those stirred by
> the lives of their predecessors? (Shi Zhecun: 'More on
> the Poems in this Magazine,' *Modern Times*, vol. 4, no.
> 1, 1933.)

This passage captures the rupture writers felt had taken place
between the pre-industrial, pre-Westernised past, and the
present. The modern, urban landscape brought about by
economic and social upheaval and a lifestyle dictated by
capitalism was well and truly here to stay. This shift towards
materialism triggered new changes in the city's literature.
Modern literature broke with its past in all aspects: in language,
turning away from the use of classical Chinese towards
vernacular Chinese; in content, turning its back on
Confucianism towards the more pragmatic concerns of
everyday life; and in structure, moving away from episodic
epics and towards more topic-centred narratives.

Whatever we think of the profligacy and materialism of
this period, it's important to remember these changes were
accompanied by breathtaking economic growth. This
simultaneous coexistence of prosperity and decadence – which
can be tentatively called the 'modern tradition' – can first be
seen in the late 19th century with works like Han Bangqing's
novel *The Sing-Song Girls of Shanghai*. It was to become perhaps

the defining feature of the avant-garde Haipai, or 'Shanghai school', during what is now regarded as the city's 'golden age' (the late 20s and 30s). This coexistence of contrasts is captured most succinctly in the opening and closing lines of Mu Shiying's short story, 'Shanghai Foxtrot': 'Shanghai. A heaven built upon a hell.' Along with other writers of this era, like Liu Na'ou, Mu Shiying was seen as belonging to a subset of the Shanghai scene called the 'New Sensational School', a group of left-wing writers frequently offering bleak, present-day dystopias of sin, corruption and debauchery.

However, the works of many modernist short story writers of this era, from Yu Dafu to Ding Ling, Jiang Guangci to Ba Jin, were in a slightly different vein. For example, the protagonists in their stories are not only beneficiaries and consumers of this new materialism, but also open critics of modernity generally, striving to offset or eradicate corruption and wrong-doing in Shanghai life wherever possible. This brings us perhaps to the second tradition in Shanghai school, which could be tentatively called the 'critical tradition', famous for its left-wing cultural standpoint and humanitarianism (see Chen Sihe, *Two traditions of Shanghai School of Literature*). Political events in the mid-1920s, which saw Nationalist, Communist, and warlord forces clashing frequently, initiated a shift to the left in Chinese writing, culminating in 1930 with the founding of the Zuoyi Zuojia Lianmeng (League of Left-Wing Writers) led by Lu Xun, who had moved from Beijing to Shanghai in 1927, famous for satirical essays (or *zawen*). Another typical example of this school of writers was the realist Mao Dun, whose best-known work, *Ziye (Midnight, 1933)* depicts the metropolitan milieu of Shanghai in all the financial and social chaos of the post-Depression era.

The thirties were the best of times and the worst of times for the city; much of the city's growth (becoming the world's

5th largest city by 1932) was due to the arrival of 70,000 foreigners (including 20,000 White Russians, and 30,000 European Jews), but in January 1932, Japanese forces invaded the city, occupying all quarters except the International Settlement (American and British concessions now combined) and the French concession, and making the lives of ordinary Chinese citizens miserable. Come December 1941, these foreign concessions also fell to Japanese rule and remained occupied until Japan's surrender in 1945.

The final liberation of Shanghai didn't come until 1949, following the People's Liberation Army's victory in the Shanghai Campaign – one of the final stages of the Civil War between the US-backed Nationalists, or 'Kuomintang', and the communists. This liberation opened a new chapter in Chinese history, which saw literature develop in an altogether new direction, following Chairman Mao Zedong's call for a truly proletarian literature – written by and for workers, peasants, and soldiers – and the arrival of Socialist Realism, a method of composition borrowed from the Soviet Union, according to which society is described as it should be, not necessarily as it is. Important writers from this period include Ru Zhijuan, who resisted the emphasis on grand narratives, and preferred to deal with the more immediate or local concerns and stories of ordinary people. A typical example of Ru Zhijuan's work is 'Lilies', the story of a newly-married wife living in the countryside, who refuses to lend her new quilt to a shy Liberation Army soldier but, by the end of the story, is placing it over the same soldier's dead body in honour of his devotion to others.

In 1978, the Chinese government announced new reforms, including the Open Door Policy, allowing foreign businesses to set up in China, and marking a complete break from the ideology of Culture Revolution. At this point, Shanghai entered a new period of 'opening up' to the outside world, reforming its economy almost beyond recognition. Shanghai became the largest economic centre in China, as well as a major financial and trading hub, which currently boasts the title of busiest port in the world. Its literature has mirrored and matched these changes. Following the Cultural Revolution, a new movement known as 'scar literature' emerged, an accusatory form of literary catharsis, followed in turn by a more professional and daring type of writing, as exemplified in the stories and plays of Bai Hua (who spent much of his life in Shanghai), known for their sharp political criticism of the previous twenty years. Writers who had been lost to earlier generations, like the essayist and screenwriter Zhang Ailing (aka Eileen Chang, who left mainland China in the mid-40s), were also rediscovered.

Come the early 1980s, China's writers were reaching huge audiences, through a wide variety of literary magazines that ran to over a million copies every issue. By the end of the decade the size of these readerships, and thus the influence of literature on society, was beginning to decline. Nonetheless, the overall scale of literary production in China remained formidable.

As this anthology demonstrates, for all its fluctuations, Shanghai writing continues to preserve certain literary traditions in the face of modernity, often with women writers at the forefront. Among these is Wang Anyi, daughter of the aforementioned Ru Zhijuan – featured here with her story 'Ah Fang's Light' – who perseveres the critical humanitarianism of the 'Shanghai School' in novellas like *Lapse in Time*, and whose work 'does not stint in describing the brutalising density, the rude jostling, the interminable and often futile waiting in line that accompany life in the big Chinese city' (to quote Jeffery Kinkley). Chen Danyan – whose story 'Snow' is featured here – is known for her romantic depictions of old Shanghai from a modern perspective, often through young, female eyes. A subset of these modern literary concerns is a focus on crises of identity brought about by rapid changes in lifestyle and generational disconnects, a theme which coincidentally also loomed large in the New Sensational School of the 1930s. Contemporary writers such as Xiao Bai and Cai Jun, whose stories 'Transparency' and 'Suzhou River' feature in this book, maintain and technologically update many of that School's concerns.

Shanghai is a typical immigrant city. Most of the early, domestic immigrants arrived from Zhejiang and Jiangsu provinces. But its allure to international migrants is still one linked to its glamorous-decadent past; an allure summed up by the title of a popular travel book published in 1937 (and still in print in Chinese): *Shanghai: The Paradise for Adventurers*. According to the census in 2018, there are 24.18 million permanent residents in Shanghai, of which 40 per cent are immigrants. Gu Lingzhou, the protagonist in Fu Yuehui's story here, 'The Lost', is a typical young 'Shanghai rover' (an immigrant from the provinces, struggling to make it in Shanghai). Generally speaking, identity depends on a continuity of human experience. It doesn't stand up well to violent and repeated severances or restarts. However, in the context of China's vast and ongoing urbanisation, the nature of identity learns to evolve from something substantial and stable to a more selective and mobile condition. Fu Yuehui explores this condition through the metaphor of losing a vital piece of modern technology, the mobile phone.

Shanghai's openness as a city has also mirrored its position as a fountainhead of formal experimentation. From the modernism of novelists like Shi Zhecun or poets like Dai Wangshu in the 1930s, to the new avant-garde of 80s writers like novelist Sun Ganlu or critic Wu Liang, the city's writers have always devoted themselves to the innovation of form. Literary experimentation, of course, goes hand-in-hand with groundbreaking subject matter, and the exploration of new and different possibilities for human existence. Chen Qiufan ('State of Trance') and Shen Dacheng ('The Novelist in the Attic') continue this literary tradition respectively, one in science fiction, the other in thriller writing.

When visiting Shanghai, people often go straight to the International Architecture Exhibition (the Bund), or to view the skyscrapers in the Lujiazui Financial District, along both sides of Huangpu River (this is also the part of the city most often seen in blockbusters films: *Skyfall, Mission: Impossible III, Transformers II,* etc.). The universal popularity of these sites among tourists reminds us of the homogeneity of globalisation. Airports, luxurious hotels, shopping malls, financial centres – these may be what most metropolises around the world have in common, what we expect to find, what we think we're coming to look at, but what's really unique about any destination is the particular outlooks of the citizens living there, the intricate, varied and often hidden historical traditions each one carries with them. Even in the same city, the economic possibilities, lifestyles and living conditions of different groups of residents are multiple, complex and widely disparate. In the war-torn Shanghai of the 40s, Eileen Chang's novels brilliantly explored the life of ordinary citizens, rather than the more commercial tendency at the time to focus on Europeanisation and the city's elites. Similarly today, writers like Teng Xiaolan ('Woman Dancing under Stars'), Xia Shang ('Bengal Tiger') and Wang Zhanhei ('The Story of Ah Ming') all strive to present close-up studies of the many varied tensions that make up urban life and the individuals navigating them. Despite being the youngest writer here (born in 1991), Wang Zhanhei refuses to take her cues from the latest consumer trends or the lifestyle fads of the city's ultra-rich *xin gui* ('new nobles') in mapping out what Shanghai is. Instead she focuses on retired workers, run-down streets, abandoned buildings, breakfast stalls at the entrance of the alleys waiting to be cleaned up. Her work brings out the inherent vitality and richness of these neglected areas and people.

After all, if this book is to offer a literary map of the city, it has to be a comprehensive one. A true map cannot simply mark out the landmarks, and the most popular tourist sites, it must be able to guide readers through the city's lesser-known corners, its dimly-lit nooks and rarely-frequented crannies. That is to say, a literary map must reveal the joys and sorrows lurking in *every* crevice of Shanghai life.

Jin Li
January, 2020

Ah Fang's Lamp

Wang Anyi

Translated by Helen Wang

PEOPLE OFTEN HAVE GREY days, just as there are sometimes grey skies.

I walked down that wet little side street, and every single door was shut. Raindrops rapped on the concrete road, rat-a-tat-tat, spattering echoes in the empty street. Gazing at the leaden cloud, the monotonous sound of rain all around, an indescribable gloom welled in my heart.

Yet on sunny days, this little street is bright and breezy. The doors of the houses are half-open, old people sit outside preparing vegetables as little children play beside them. Behind the quiet old people and the lively little ones are their family homes. What kind of lives go on in these homes that open on to the street? When I have time to spare, and nothing else on my mind, I start to wonder.

On one particular day, a very ordinary day – not grey, but not one of those cloudless days either – I was walking along and, by a chance turn of the head, caught a glimpse through an open door. Although it was way past lunchtime, the table hadn't been cleared, and a big man lay sprawled over a bamboo couch, so dead to the world that the fly on his cheek looked completely at ease. An old woman, apparently his mother, had her back to the door, and was working the treadle of a heavy sewing machine, the crude sound of which drowned out his

1

snoring. Everything inside was unutterably decrepit, and when I caught a whiff of decay, I stopped looking and walked on. The evening sun dazzled on the wutong leaves, and I walked on through leaf-mottled shadows.

Time passed, and I found myself walking up and down this street several times a day. I had moved house, and it turned out that the street was on my way to work. After walking this way for I don't know how long, I began to notice a tiny fruit stall set out beneath a window. The window- and door-frames had a fresh coat of red-brown paint, and there was a big green fibreglass canopy over the window. Beside the stall sat a girl with Japanese style hair, her thick fringe masking lively eyes. Her face was beautifully delicate, if a little too pale, but her lips were naturally red and full. She wore a red jacket, and like a red cloud that had settled beside the yellow pears, green apples and black water chestnuts, she would sit there quietly reading a small illustrated book or knitting a jumper that was not just red. When someone walked past, her eyes would peer up through the black hair on her forehead, and as soon as the person slowed their step, she would be on her feet, waiting quietly but keenly. The waiting paid off; people rarely disappointed.

On one occasion, I stopped in front of her fruit stall and she called me over: 'Come and buy something!' Her voice was coarse and gravelly, completely at odds with her delicate appearance. I was there for a while, and, assuming I was trying to make up my mind, she said, 'The Hami melons are very good, they just arrived at Shiliupu Wharf yesterday. They're a little pricey, but they're worth it.'

I didn't buy a melon, but after I'd selected a few apples and she held up the scales, I noticed her hands. Her knobbly joints and dry palms spoke silently of a hard life. And yet her face was so young, her soft, smooth cheeks so white and translucent, her eyes so bright. She weighed the apples, then worked out the price on a tiny calculator, her thick finger tapping on keys the size of rice grains, rounded it down, and helped me put the apples in my bag.

After dark, business would be brisker, and a man came to help her. I heard him call her Ah Fang. I guessed he was her husband, though I felt she was far too young to have one. Then one day, I noticed there was something different about Ah Fang. It took me a few walks up and down the street to work it out. When I realised that her waist had thickened, and it was clear that she was pregnant, a strange feeling welled up inside me; I felt sorry for her, but also moved. And when I looked at the two of them again, I couldn't deny they looked good together. He was a big strong man, she was a beautiful slim woman, and they were both young. You couldn't not feel happy for them. He wasn't as quick with his hands as Ah Fang, and he wasn't as sharp as her either, but he was just as attentive to the customers. One evening, he tried to get me to buy some bananas that were past their best, and followed me down the street for a while in the light rain, saying over and over again:

'You can pay later if you don't have the cash on you now.'

Another time, when I was buying lychees, Ah Fang started a conversation:

'I always see you walking up and down. You must live on this street. Which number are you?'

I told her that I didn't live on that street, and that I had to walk this way every day to work.

'I thought that might be the case' she said, helping me with the lychees. I noticed a dark patch on her face, and a dullness about her lips. But she'd painted her nails with bright red polish. Although they were at odds with her thick finger joints, and inevitably tacky, there was an innocence to them, and I didn't find them at all repulsive. In return, I asked her a question:

'Who brings the fruit here? You surely don't do it all by yourself?'

'My husband does it. He goes to Shiliupu after work, or sometimes first thing in the morning.'

'And the licence is in your name?'

'Yes, although technically I'm unemployed!' The brown mark on her face seemed to redden as she answered, so I didn't ask any more.

It seemed that Ah Fang and her fruit stall had brought new life to this street, even on days when dark clouds filled the sky.

Late one night, when it was raining lightly, I walked this way and found the entire street was quiet, with all the doors closed. In the distance, I saw an electric lamp hanging in front of Ah Fang's door, shining down on her belly as she sat in her chair, head lowered, knitting a sweater. I didn't want to startle her, and continued to walk on the other side of the street. As I walked slowly past, her exquisite profile across the wet street moved across my line of vision.

After that, the fruit stall was packed away, presumably around the time Ah Fang gave birth. The street became unusually quiet and cold. Not just on overcast days, but on bright sunny days too. Ah Fang's door was closed. The closing of the door, like a drop of water running into the sea, returned the house to the long row of doors that all looked the same. I couldn't even remember which was Ah Fang's door, and made a mental note, next time the door was open, to record the house number above the door lintel. But, in such a vast world, what does a little character like Ah Fang count for? After I'd walked past a few more times, this young woman faded from my thoughts, and I got used to this watery street not having a fruit stall. It was just a street I walked through, my life being something that happened at either end. And as far as the street was concerned, I was just a passerby, the different lives inside those different doors were none of my business.

I continued to walk through that street every day, knowing the square concrete blocks that made up the road like the back of my hand. Green bamboo poles poked out of open windows that looked on to the street, bearing washing hung out to dry; ice-cold drops of water collecting in the corners of these clothes seemed to fall on my forehead with a cheeky familiarity. Sometimes, there'd be rainbow soap bubbles floating in the air. I'd catch one in the palm of my hand, and it would stay for a while, like a dream shining back at me. A child's dream, I thought, and then it would burst without a sound, leaving the slipperiness of water in my palm. Then a new one, even prettier, would float down towards me. From winter to summer, autumn to spring, there were grey days, and bright days, and I came to be so familiar with the street I didn't notice it any more. Although there was that one time, when a dark red rose branch torn from its bush suddenly fell from one of the roofs on to my shoulder, then landed at my feet. It was a very clear early morning just after a Category-10 typhoon. It was as though I had received a message and set me wondering about Ah Fang. *She must be a mother by now,* I thought. Did she have a boy or a girl? She probably wouldn't be opening the fruit stall anymore!

But Ah Fang did set out her fruit stall again. One evening, no different from all the other evenings before it, I suddenly noticed her. With the same fringe over her eyes, which were as bright as ever, and still wearing a red jacket, her skin just as white and translucent as before, she was quietly running a fruit stall ablaze with purples and reds. Only now she had a fat white baby in her arms, with lips as red as her own. The slender Ah Fang with a fat white baby in her arms looked adorable. She apparently didn't recognise me when she called out attentively:

'Come, take your pick?'

When I'd selected a bunch of bananas, she put the child in

a stroller in front of the door, and weighed the bananas. I noticed a new thick band of gold on her ring finger, which had a rich, dark gleam to it.

The street had a fruit stall again. Ah Fang was back, with her husband and baby. Ah Fang finally recognised me, or at least said she remembered me. Whenever I passed by she would greet me and encourage me to buy something, or ask if yesterday's melon had been sweet or not. I was welcome to buy on credit, she would tell me, though I never did.

The little boy started to grow, gradually, almost imperceptibly; and Ah Fang, also gradually and imperceptibly, started to put on weight, though she was still slim and beautiful. Another heavy gold necklace appeared around her neck, and she wore a delicate little bracelet on her wrist. In the evenings, under the electric lamp they brought outside, Ah Fang knitted sweaters, her husband read books, and her toddler learned to walk in a baby walker. The fruit on the stall changed with the seasons, and there would often be some more exotic, and more expensive, fruits, such as mangoes, sitting regally among the crowd of ordinary fruit.

This picture of simplicity and harmony often touched me, offering a sense of the power of life in its most ideal form, a glimpse into the secret of life and of living. On those miserable drizzly days, those frustrating and anxious days, the sight of Ah Fang, even the dull glow of the lamp by her door, was enough to lift my spirits.

One night, there was an almighty downpour that saw rain bouncing off the ground. With almost no one out on the street, bicycles flew past in the blink of an eye. As I passed Ah Fang's door, there was an emptiness around it, although the door itself was open and a light on inside. All of a sudden, I heard someone call me; in the clatter of rain, it seemed far away. But when I looked round, I saw Ah Fang's husband, standing in the doorway. They had the most delicious muskmelon that day, he said; he'd give a refund if it wasn't sweet; or I could take it, eat it, and pay later, and so on and so on. I smiled at him, collapsed my umbrella and went in. The toddler was asleep, his head sticking out from beneath a pink blanket, his fingers in his mouth. Ah Fang was watching TV, a live Yueju opera contest, on a 20-inch colour TV. Inside there was a refrigerator, a twin-tub washing machine, a ceiling fan, a cassette recorder, and so on. I chose a muskmelon from the basket, and after I'd paid for it, Ah Fang's husband invited me to sit for a while, until the rain stopped.

The rain was torrential. Bucketing it down, as they say. I didn't go, but I didn't sit either, continuing to stand there chatting with him.

'Are there just the three of you living here?' I asked.

Yes, he said, his mother had died last year, adding that she used to sleep upstairs.

I hadn't noticed there was an upstairs, but halfway down the room was a sliding wooden door, carefully painted a cream colour, which was closed.

'And your fruit business is doing well?' I asked.

'It's unpredictable,' he said. 'Take last summer's watermelons, we had so many of them, then it turned cold and the price dropped just like that, and we lost hundreds, you know! But the state-run stores lost even more,' he laughed, taking comfort in the thought. I found that, despite his stocky build, there was a bookish air about him, as though he'd had an education. I asked him what he did, and he said he was just a lathe operator, that he'd taken over his mother's job at the factory when he came back from the countryside.

A thought flashed through my mind, as I suddenly remembered, all those years ago, walking around here, that messy, bleak scene through the door. There was a son and a mother. Perhaps it was this place, right here, it must have been here. My mind started spinning. Ah Fang was singing along with a contestant – 'Baoyu's Tears of Grief' – and was too absorbed to care about a stranger in the midst. I looked at her, and wondered if she had pulled that bleak home back from the brink? If she had turned the jaded lives of a mother and son around, and restored their honour?

But I didn't know for sure if that was this place. All the doors here look the same, and when they're shut, you can't tell whose is whose. I desperately wanted confirmation, but feared it at the same time. I was afraid that my speculation would be unfounded, like a dream being shattered. I wanted it to be that home, I wanted it with all my heart. So I decided to leave straight away. The rain was pelting down, even heavier than before. Ah Fang's husband did his best to make me stay, and even Ah Fang herself looked round and said, 'Stay a while.'

But I still left.

I ran from Ah Fang's home as though I was running away. Ah Fang's lamp in the doorway cast a dim light a good length of the way. I didn't look back. I was afraid I'd be unable to resist asking for, and getting, confirmation, and it was so unnecessary and stupid. I didn't want to spoil this beautiful story, I wanted it to live on, with me.

And that was how I wove my own beautiful fairy tale, which, on grey or rainy days, inspires me not to be disheartened. And I have written this story down, word by word, sentence by sentence, in the wish that it will become a little tale told of this little street, for Ah Fang's toddler when he grows up, and forever in the future.

Snow

Chen Danyan

Translated by Paul Harris

EARLY ONE NEW YEAR'S morning Zheng Ling hastily put on her make-up and, carrying a pile of parcels of varying sizes, pulled shut the security door of her apartment. Her husband had already been waiting in the lift for some time, keeping his finger on the 'Door Open' button. He had to be on duty today, while she was expected at her parents' house. She was taking them an old heavy thermos bucket packed with spicy stewed fish, spare-ribs with carrots braised in soya sauce, and twice-cooked pork, all prepared by her Szechwan maid. The red plastic thermos bucket had been bought at the time that her mother had been in hospital, and it was never used on ordinary occasions. Zheng Ling, along with her elder brother and younger sister, had agreed to take food to celebrate the New Year with their parents. In her handbag she also carried a bulky, half-read French novel, plus a black Moleskin notebook. While reading, she liked to jot down notes, the way solitary readers often do, as if they know they're never going to find any like-minded soul to share their thoughts with about what they've read but need to confide them in writing all the same.

During the few minutes the lift was descending Zheng Ling sighed audibly and confessed to her husband: 'I'm worried what sort of state I'll find Mum in when I get there.' She could have waited for her brother to collect their father from his long-stay hospital before going to her parents' place, so she wouldn't be alone with her. But her husband had to start his shift at eight o'clock, so she had to set off with him now. 'Why not sit in the coffeehouse around the corner from theirs for a bit and relax with a nice book?' her husband suggested, to allay her fears.

Pushing open the main door of the apartment building, they saw it was raining. The tops of the evergreen camphor trees were shrouded in a damp grey fog. During the past few days foggy weather had been causing traffic chaos up and down the country, and there was constant talk on the news about overcrowded long-distance bus stations and airports. Looking at the damp fog, Zheng Ling thought: *Lucky for me I don't have to be stuck in one of those smelly waiting-rooms. If it were me, I'd go mad.* Then she remembered how a friend of hers had once described a foggy day. This was a woman who had suddenly discovered a passion for Chinese culture and started going to Peking operas, took up the Chinese zither and read books written in the old-style Chinese language. One day they were eating together in a Vietnamese restaurant in Gubei, a classy quarter in Shanghai. Leaning her elbows on the dinner table and looking outside, her friend had said, 'A foggy day like this must be what they used to call a ...' and she mentioned a literary term that referred to a dense mist containing particles of dust. Zheng Ling thought of this now, but in her view there was nothing poetical about it.

The streets were murky and the houses on either side were sunk in silence this early on New Year's Day. It was a peculiar kind of silence, accompanied by a feeling that always came over her first thing in the morning of a public holiday before a family get-together, a sort of sinking of the heart, mingled with a nervous tension, as if you were being pressured to be happy and satisfied with life. 'I wonder why Mum is so unhappy and dissatisfied,' Zheng Ling said bitterly. The past year had brought a succession of crises for the family. Zheng Ling's aged father had been dangerously ill, but his condition had now stabilised. In the autumn her mother had needed an urgent operation. That had been a particularly difficult time. Her mother had suffered from depression for many years, and the children had been worried sick that the operation might make her worse. So, in spite of arranging 24-hour nursing care for her, they had still taken it in turns to look after her. But their mother had now recovered. So looking back as the year was coming to an end, they had reason to feel grateful. Zheng Ling would soon be turning fifty, and she still had Mum and Dad around, people who still used pet names in the way they addressed her. If she thought things through, she had to admit that she was fortunate. And yet she dreaded the prospect of going to see her mother who, despite taking such good care of her skin, always looked miserable. *That downcast 'female intellectual of a certain age' look*, Zheng Ling thought, *And on a lifeless morning like this, I really need something to cheer me up.*

Their old Buick cruised along the highway, sweeping past a vast reddish-brown building. Zheng Ling's health club was on the third storey. Twice a week she attended yoga classes there and once a week went swimming. By the window of the brightly lit gym a woman was busy on the jogging machine, her short light-brown hair bobbing up and down. Zheng Ling guessed who it was: one of her fellow yoga students, Chief Chinese Representative for a foreign company, unmarried, very fastidious. She was at the gym every day but would never use the bath towel provided. After taking a shower, she would take a whole lot of face tissues and dab at the drops of water on her body. Although Zheng Ling was sure she wasn't doing this to get attention, it still got on her nerves. To insist on going to the gym for an early morning jog on a day like this just showed how lonely she was, in Zheng Ling's view. And this made her feel uncomfortable.

Because of their mother's long-term depression and obsession with cleanliness, Zheng Ling and her siblings had become sensitive to their mother's moods and took great care not to irritate her. If their father's doctor hadn't said he could go home for a day, they probably wouldn't have bothered their mother with the visit. But perhaps each one of them was thinking that this might be the last occasion for such a gathering, and so they all had to be there, no matter what. Perhaps they all felt that God was allowing them this last opportunity for a family get-together. They wouldn't say so openly, of course.

'I'm afraid this will be our family's last time together. It's a pity the children can't get back,' Zheng Ling said to her husband, meaning their daughter and her elder brother's child, who were both studying in America and would probably not even be celebrating Chinese New Year. Her husband didn't reply. His father had died nearly twenty years before. His mother was still alive, but not very happy. She had kept the last poem his father had written for her just before he died: 'May you live to reach a ripe old age and then be my comfort in the other world.' The first New Year after he passed away his mother had gone away on holiday, to stop herself from fretting at home. There had been three children in both Zheng Ling's and her husband's families, the youngest being a daughter in each case. Her husband and his siblings had taken advantage of their mother's absence at New Year to go through their father's things. Zheng Ling had been pregnant with their daughter at the time, so just sat by and watched. In the drawer of their father's desk, they happened across a notebook containing poems written in slightly leftward-sloping characters. They stood in silence at the desk staring intently at the short lines of old-fashioned verse. Everyone used to say her husband's parents were devoted to each other. Sitting there on the sofa looking at the three siblings, Zheng Ling thought, *Children of a happy family, but now they're suffering for it.*

'Your mum and dad have both reached an advanced age,' her husband said.

'But I haven't made any preparations for when they go.'

'Who on earth can?' her husband replied. Zheng Ling remembered that when her father-in-law died, her husband had hurried home on just such a foggy morning in search of a shirt to dress his father's body in, before taking it to the crematorium. At that time she was still living near her parents, who were so worried that her husband, in such an agitated state, might have an accident, that they decided to fetch a white shirt to the hospital themselves. They also accompanied her mother-in-law on the day, when she went to say the last goodbye.

'The best plan for today,' her husband suggested, 'would be to take my mum to your mum's place. At least that way everyone can be together.'

'I'm not sure if my mum would like that. She can be so difficult and unwelcoming,' Zheng Ling confessed. She visualised the round face of her mother-in-law, who had the same downcast female intellectual look as her mother. She too suffered from depression, took Prozac and was always moaning. An ice-cold feeling came over Zheng Ling as she added resignedly, 'But I suppose we could try.'

They had entered the narrow streets of the old part of the city: Xingguo Road, Wukang Road and Yongfu Road. The several-storied buildings of the old concession quarter were drenched after the overnight rain. Their long-since redundant chimneys, which looked about to topple over, protruded from the red-tiled sloping roofs. Zheng Ling breathed in the sense of tranquillity in decay she was so familiar with. This was the part of the city she had grown up in. In her present, semi-wakeful state, she felt like she was back home. The French bakery on the corner was ablaze with lights. Through the coffeehouse windows you could see in the lounge all the chairs upside down on the tables. The words 'Merry Xmas and Happy New Year' in English were still glittering in silver tinfoil letters over the bar. Christian pastors used to take exception to the way the younger generation and non-believers omitted 'Christ' from Christmas and abbreviated it to 'X'. But Zheng Ling was particularly fond of this 'X'. To her it embodied the confusion that many people felt deep down about Christmas and how it had been spoilt by commercialisation. It was how she felt about it too.

'So where are you going to while away the next couple of hours then?' her husband asked. A large gathering was expected at her mother's place around ten, so Zheng Ling wouldn't have to be on the receiving end of her mother's complaining on her own. Her husband had his fair share of the same from his own mother, of course, so he well understood Zheng Ling's dread. Besides, he was also used to Zheng Ling's complaining. With the brown leather steering wheel between his hands, he just wanted to calm her down, so that he could spend a quiet day by himself at the office. 'The coffeehouse isn't open,' Zheng Ling said. 'Only KFC's open.'

She usually only went to a coffeehouse after lunch, to read. She always came to this district. She would spend the whole afternoon here before returning home, frequently passing the big iron door of her mother's place on the way, but rarely looking in. In her favourite coffeehouse she had a favourite seat. She usually ordered a white coffee and would afterwards ask for a glass of water. Once it started getting dark, she would order a small piece of cheesecake. Its sweetness cheered her up at that time of day, lifted her sagging spirits amid the gathering gloom, together with the warmth of the place, its aroma, the sound of other customers, and the music. She loved listening to unfamiliar music. Everything in the coffeehouse made her feel at ease: being with lots of people, enjoying the noise of their lively chatter. It didn't disturb her at all. In her husband's eyes she too was a female intellectual with an obsession with cleanliness, always looking for something to moan about.

Zheng Ling reflected that for her, a woman, to be reading on her own in a fried-chicken restaurant early on New Year's Day must appear unnatural. She remembered the solitary figure on the jogging machine and realised that the contempt she had felt for her was not because of the face tissues but because the woman was doing nothing to conceal her loneliness as a single person, in the same way that the women in the changing room who used to strip to the buff also disgusted her. Ever since her daughter had left home to go to university, Zheng Ling had felt a strong aversion to lonely women. She also felt a profound sense of shame. Loneliness seemed to her a symbol of failure, of rejection. It struck her incidentally that using KFC as a refuge to read in might be even worse than jogging in the gym first thing in the morning. She had kept these feelings to herself when in the car. It was difficult to talk about such things to a husband so tied up with his work.

She had now arrived at her mother's. Next to the old green iron door was the paulownia tree she used to pass every day when she was little. It was wreathed in the dense fog of that New Year morning and reminded her of a chopstick standing in thick noodle soup. She was suddenly startled by a memory of her childhood loneliness. Those dreary New Years, when her father was never at home and no relatives called. Her mother hated having visitors over and struggled to be agreeable to other people. Their kitchen was never like others', with the smell of cooking and all sorts of goodies to eat. In winter it was always foggy outside and freezing indoors. Through the glass window, which seemed paper-thin in the cold weather, the young Zheng Ling used to gaze at the trees, darkened by fog, and imagine how behind the windows opposite, dripping with condensation, a happy party was in progress. Beside a table piled with all sorts of presents and emptied tea-cups, people like her would be bustling about and enjoying the kind of jokes that no-one outside their family would understand.

Zheng Ling finally made up her mind. She would go to the KFC at the end of the street and wait there a couple of hours. As she expected, there were no other customers. But it was warm and dry at least. She ordered a cup of scalding hot Hong Kong tea with milk and took it to a corner nestled between three walls. As she made herself comfortable, some other customers came into the restaurant. The soft voice of the young woman ordering a breakfast soothed Zheng Ling's nerves. She heard the two of them sit down not far from where she sat and, when they spoke, realised that the companion was a young man. They were discussing their parents and relatives. Zheng Ling recognised the tone of resignation in their voices. She remembered it was how she used to feel at New Year in the days before she was married. But what irked her then was not her parents or relatives as such, but the psychological pressure that seemed to always accompany public holidays. So here were others trying to escape the vexations of family gatherings early on New Year's Day – just like her. Zheng Ling took a sip from her cup of scalding hot tea. Recently she had developed a liking for drinking tea and coffee before it cooled. She liked the feel of the hot liquid slithering down her throat into her stomach. It was somehow like when you ironed a pair of still damp cotton trousers. It gave her a reassuring sense of things being as they should be.

Zheng Ling took out her novel and her notebook and put on her glasses. The novel was set in German-occupied France and was about a love affair between a German soldier and a French village girl. It was a sad and emotionally charged story. Its impact was reinforced when you knew that the author herself, a French Jewish woman, had been in hiding in the countryside in the south of France. The novel, with its realistic and neatly constructed plot, was written while she was trying to escape detection by the authorities, and after she had written the very last word she was transported to Poland where she died. When you considered all this and how up to the very end she could still write with such human insight and an absence of any resentment or prejudice, the power of her vision was all the more impressive. A good novel will always make you, the reader, relate it to events in your own experience. As the story develops, so do you. But if you are walking along a narrow path lined with rose bushes, what you notice is not the path, but the roses on either side, the flowers in full bloom, which are part of your own experience. What you see, through the novel, is your own life and yourself.

Like a rubber ball in water, Zheng Ling was carried along by the story. She had loved novels ever since she was a young girl. She used to go to bed early and sit on the quilt with a book in her hands. Bathed in the yellow halo from her reading lamp and immersed in the story, she felt as safe as if she were sitting inside a dome-shaped mosquito net. This had always been one of Zheng Ling's favourite occupations. Sometimes, when she had a novel in her hands, her imagination would summon up sounds she had heard when reading in the past, such as the son next door practising the clarinet, with the music reminding her of black grapes rolling around a table-top, or the sound of the radio jamming when her father was trying to listen to Voice of America, or downstairs' baby crying. He was a sickly child, who was put out in the sun during the day. He had lost a lot of hair from the back of his head and his scalp was covered in white scales, while the skin under his eyes was an unhealthy green. These were the sounds of her family home, sounds she'd been so familiar with all her life. With her memories of that home still so vivid, Zheng Ling couldn't believe that she had nearly passed the half-way point of her life. Going back to the district where she had grown up felt like returning to where she naturally belonged. This old district had retained an atmosphere redolent of the faded bourgeoisie. With today's Shanghai spawning so many more fashionable quarters, this district seemed a backwater by comparison, yet it carried on in its own quiet unhurried way. Zheng Ling thought that if she had still been in her thirties, perhaps she would have liked the Xintiandi and Gubei districts of Shanghai, but now she only really felt at home in these grey, old streets, with their decaying apartments dating back to the 1920s, the old Western-style buildings of the 1940s, and the paulownia trees that were planted all round here in the 1970s. She cherished those derelict and redundant chimneys protruding from red-tiled roofs and the wisteria stretching out its shoots from low garden walls. The French novel she was reading made her visualise the road outside. She could imagine herself travelling such a road into exile, as if she too would soon be on her way to Poland to die.

On the pavement outside the window an elderly woman was passing slowly. She turned her pale round face towards the restaurant. It was sad and drawn. For a moment, Zheng Ling thought it was her mother and her heart missed a beat. The woman was wearing a pair of exquisite brown shoes and a reddish-brown woollen jacket. They were in a style that was now out of fashion, but it was how a well-dressed woman of the previous generation would have looked. She was carrying some milk she had evidently just bought and, glancing at her through the window, Zheng Ling thought she looked bad-tempered. Zheng Ling had often noticed how many more sad-looking faces there were among the old people here than in the new district where she lived, not like the easy-going look of those you saw walking with their children in the new districts. Most of those round here, like her own parents, lived in old houses with unoccupied floors full only of memories of those who had since moved on. In their storerooms they would keep their children's chests, along with their old bedclothes, a violin or an accordion. These old people living on their own, weren't they perhaps the ones with the greater self-respect. Or were they also just a hangover from the bourgeois past? Although Zheng Ling was afraid of getting involved with people of that generation, deep down she admired them. But then she remembered how annoying she found old people who seemed happy to spend day after day gathered around the courtyard fountain, keeping the children amused. Their smiling faces and their chatter brought to mind the expression 'old biddies'. She knew she was being harsh and unreasonable thinking of them this way, but she couldn't help it. She watched as the shrivelled figure dressed in light brown passed a 1940s Spanish-style building. That was the nursery school Zheng Ling had attended as a child. She then crossed a Western-style street also dating from the 1940s. That was where her primary school teacher had lived. The elderly woman turned into the street opposite, which was where Zheng Ling and her boyfriend used to meet. There was a small shop that sold pirate CDs. The proprietor was a fan of Western opera and would be forever playing Puccini. Zheng Ling remembered that in spring and summer you could hear arias from *Madame Butterfly* halfway down the street. The soaring notes of the soprano singing 'One Fine Day' would still be following you when you were quite a distance away. It lifted your spirits, although, in actual fact, fine days in Shanghai were something of a rarity.

It suddenly struck Zheng Ling: *I wonder what that lady with the milk thinks of me, a woman on her own sitting in an American fried-chicken restaurant, drinking tea early on New Year's morning. Perhaps the same thoughts are going through her head as I had when I caught sight from the car of the woman jogging in the health club. Perhaps I make her feel uncomfortable.*

'I'm fed up to the back teeth', the young girl was saying. Even in the company of the young man, you could tell from her voice she was lonely and depressed. Like an echo in an empty room, Zheng Ling felt her gentle young voice touch a string deep inside her. 'I hate these dreary days. Just hate them.' Like a feather fluttering down, her voice echoed softly inside Zheng Ling. 'Am I turning into a misery, like Mum?' she asked.

In the novel Zheng Ling was reading, the young French country girl was madly in love with the German officer billeted with her family. Meanwhile the catastrophe that would engulf the novel's Jewish author was gradually approaching. The book's flyleaf showed a facsimile of her manuscript, which had the effect of confronting the reader with the full force of what was to come, like the second subject in the movement of a symphony.

All of a sudden someone in the restaurant cried out in excitement, 'It's snowing!'

It was snowing. Zheng Ling saw fine white flakes falling from the grey sky. They were faint, but coming fast. The old buildings opposite had become indistinct, like a dream landscape in an impressionist painting. Pedestrians on the street were looking up at the sky as they walked, with a smile of enchantment on their faces, as if they could not believe the fluttering snow was real. The two lovers sitting next to Zheng Ling abandoned a tableful of food and rushed outside, the girl in her thin, grey tight-fitting sweater. The heavy snow made her look very slim, and Zheng Ling saw her face gradually redden in the cold bracing air, like a shiny bright apple.

Zheng Ling got up and went out too. All around there was a smell of fresh cold snow and the freezing air soon penetrated her thin sweater making her flesh tingle. She couldn't help smiling. The street was already white. So were the sloping roofs. The early morning fog had dispersed. Between earth and sky there was nothing but snow falling continuously. She thought of the courtyard of her mother's house, which would certainly also be covered in white and where the leaves of the evergreen trees, motionless, would have caught the snowflakes, the way they did when she was a child. It was wonderful how snow always made people look happier and more friendly, covering the world until everything was white and new.

Zheng Ling stood at the street corner and gazed up Huating Road. Without a soul on the streets, all was virgin snow, not a single footprint. With their ornament of snow, even the old nineteen-twenties window ledges and roofs looked new. She remembered how the streets had looked when she was a child, and they didn't seem to have changed at all. She felt a gradual resurgence of the feelings she had known as a child, a mixture of curiosity and yearning. They had not changed either. They were still as undefined as before. Although she had been lonely as a child, she had nurtured vague hopes back then that things would somehow be better when she grew up. Everything would get better. As a child, she had always wandered about the neighbouring streets on her own and had always got wet when it snowed. Her feet would freeze in her pigskin boots. But it had always fascinated her the way the streets appeared in the snow. She considered herself lonely as an adult, too, who was forever longing inwardly for change, but never having the opportunity to achieve it, except when she was reading. But those hopes were not yet dead. Deep down, she still harboured them. In the snow Zheng Ling found, to her surprise, that she was examining herself, and amazingly the young hopes she had cherished over all those years were as fresh as ever.

She saw in the distance the entrance to a TB clinic. The elderly lady in the light-brown jacket was also standing in the snow, looking up and letting the snowflakes fall on her face. It reminded Zheng Ling of the way her mother's puppy always used to look up, her eyes so expectant.

Bengal Tiger

Xia Shang

Translated by Lee Anderson

1

'*FATHER? FATHER?*' ROCKY SAID. 'Baba, I'm talking to you.'

'Who is this "Fazer"? What are you going on about?' Chang Jing muttered, not bothering to turn around.

'"*Father*" means baba. Baba means "*father*". That's what my teacher said,' Rocky explained.

Chang Jing paused, chopsticks mid-air. 'Right, so you're just showing off your English.'

'Don't be mad, Baba. I didn't really see anything today.'

Chang Jing buried his head back in the paper, tears suddenly pricking his eyes. Eventually, with a sniffle, he got up and went to the bathroom, making sure to lock the door behind him.

Rocky followed and leant against the doorframe. 'Baba,' he called out, 'do you think there's a reason why we're alive?'

Chang Jing felt his heart skip a beat; this isn't the kind of thing you expect to hear from a young boy's mouth. Before he could say anything, Rocky answered for him: 'Cos I don't think so. I'd rather be a bird flying way up in the sky.'

'Rocky,' Chang Jing said, 'do you think your dad's a coward?'

Silence. Chang Jing splashed his face with cold water and stepped out of the bathroom. Rocky was back in the living room, flicking through TV channels. He came to a stop on one showing cartoons.

Rocky turned to look at his father and said, 'Did you just ask me something, Baba?'

'No, nothing,' Chang Jing replied, wiping his hands on his clothes.

Rocky turned his attention back to his TV programme. Minutes passed before Chang Jing blurted out again, 'Rocky, do you think I'm a coward?'

Instead of answering directly, Rocky seemed to suddenly remember something and said, 'Oh yeah, I beat up Li Chao today.'

'You mean Li Dabing's son?' Chang Jing asked, shocked. 'Why?'

'I was lying to you just now,' Rocky said, casually. 'I saw everything, actually. And if Li Dabing ever treats you like that again, I'm gonna beat his son up every single day.'

Chang Jing stared at his son, dumbfounded.

Rocky continued, 'There was another reason I beat him up, actually. He said something about our family owing his family a life... So, of course, I had to deck him.'

The words hit Chang Jing like a slap in the face, but he quickly regained composure and said, 'He was just talking nonsense. Don't take it seriously.'

A couple of minutes passed and Chang Jing announced, 'I'm off out to buy some cigs. Mum'll be back soon, you can both start eating without me.'

There was an obvious flaw in this – the corner shop was just down the street, so if Chang Jing really were just buying cigarettes, it would have only taken him five minutes or so. He was clearly up to something else. But Rocky was too engrossed in his cartoons to think too much about what his dad was saying; he simply grunted in acknowledgement, eyes glued to the screen.

Chang Jing walked down the road leading through Zoo Village, bought a pack of cigarettes from the corner shop and, instead of going back home, turned and began heading southeast towards another apartment block.

When the zoo first built this 'village' back in the mid-1960s there were only two apartment buildings, which were designed to provide free accommodation for zoo employees and their families. As the zoo expanded, and its workforce along with it, five more buildings were gradually added. In the early 1990s, the entire estate was converted into a public residential area. Commercial housing sprang up and slowly engulfed the seven original buildings, and the area was officially named Yihua Village. But old habits die hard, and the locals continued to refer to it as Zoo Village. Bus stop names weren't updated, and conductors would never use the village's new name when announcing the stops.

Upon reaching the building, Chang Jing lit a cigarette, took two puffs and flicked it away. Then up he went, coming to a stop outside Flat 303. He didn't knock straight away; he was thinking about what his opening line should be.

He decided the best course of action would be to cut right to the chase.

So he cleared his throat, took a deep breath, and yelled at the top of his lungs, 'Li Dabing, you get the hell out here right now!'

The door opened slightly, and the head of the man he was looking for emerged through the crack, grains of rice stuck to the corners of his mouth. Chang Jing recoiled instinctively. In all these years he had never once stood up to this guy, despite being almost twice his height, and despite everyone in the zoo knowing Li Dabing regarded him as a sworn enemy and would do anything he could to make his life miserable. He had especially failed to stand up to him a few years back when Dabing was promoted to a senior management position, and promptly plucked Chang Jing out of Human Resources and reassigned him as a tiger trainer. Chang Jing had not put up a fight and just gritted his teeth, so everyone now thought of him as a coward, regardless of his hulking frame. With this, though, he'd finally snapped. He didn't care if other people thought he was a coward, but he *did* care if his own son did. His voice rising, heart thumping and eyes blazing, he thundered, 'I've got a bone to pick with you. Who owes your family a life?'

Li Dabing's wife, Chen Cuiping, and their son Li Chao also poked their heads through the door. Cuiping, seeing the fury on Chang Jing's face, froze for an instant before quickly retracting her and Li Chao's heads back inside.

'You've been against me every step of the way these past few years,' Chang Jing went on, 'and I've not said a word. That doesn't mean I'm afraid of you. Think about it – I'm not scared of tigers, so would I really be scared of you?'

Chang Jing was anxious to press home the point that he didn't give Li Dabing a second thought, and that his submissiveness over the years had nothing to do with fear.

Li Dabing cleared his throat and said, 'Chang Jing, if you have something to say, can't it wait till we get to the office tomorrow? I'm just having dinner.'

'If that's all you've got to say, then I'm sorry for this,' Chang Jing replied.

Before Dabing could say another word, his face was split open like a pumpkin. He brought his hands up to feel his nose, and they came back down covered in blood. The sound of glass shattering on the floor told him his glasses were also broken.

There was a second of complete stillness, before Li Chao hopped out of the doorway like a flea and bit down on Chang Jing's left leg. Chang Jing winced, then jiggled his leg to shake the boy off like a fallen leaf.

Li Dabing's wife finally joined the fray, scooping up Li

Chao and exclaiming, 'Chang Jing, what do you think you're doing?!'

For an instant, it looked like she was about to admit something, but then thought better of it and scurried back inside with her son. Li Chao's whiny, prepubescent voice piped up from the hallway: 'You're a murderer. Your family owes my family a life.'

'You've heard it yourself now,' Chang Jing sneered. 'I think you owe me an explanation.'

'He didn't get that from either of us – he must have picked it up from somewhere else. You must know there are loads of people in the village who think that, so he must have overheard someone running their mouth off,' Dabing said, one hand cupped over his nose.

'I think you're the one who's been running his mouth off,' Chang Jing retorted. 'Sure, lots of people know what happened, but no one goes around saying that the Changs owe the Li family a life. It's not exactly the kind of thing you'd just say out loud, is it?'

Quite a crowd of zoo workers and their families had gathered in the corridor and stairwell by this point, but not one of them stepped forward to say anything, preferring to watch from a safe distance instead.

Li Dabing said, 'Well if that's what you want to think, there's not much I can do to change your mind. I must say, I never saw you as the type who'd just go around punching people. Although, if you were a real man, you'd have killed me instead.'

'If I'd have done that, I'd owe your family two lives then wouldn't I?'

Li Dabing scanned the familiar faces of those who had congregated in the entrance to the stairwell and thrust a finger in the direction of a middle-aged man wearing a khaki green jacket. 'Wu Guilong, what are you just standing there for? Aren't you the Deputy Security Manager?'

Wu Guilong emerged sheepishly from the crowd and replied, 'I don't think I should get involved, Vice Secretary Li. You're senior management and he's an ordinary employee, so someone's gonna get mad whatever side I come down on. I think it's best if you call the police.'

'But you saw him hit me, regardless,' Dabing protested. 'Surely that on its own is something security should deal with?'

'I still think this is a matter for the police... This is your home, it isn't the workplace, so people will talk if we interfere here.'

'Well, you'd best hurry up and call the police then.'

Guilong went over to Dabing and whispered something in his ear. Dabing rolled his eyes, grumbling 'You and your schemes!', then shouted back into the flat for Cuiping to call the police to report an assault.

2

Rocky was sat waiting impatiently at the dinner table, stomach growling until, unable to wait any longer, he stole a bite of pork belly. It was at this moment that Tong Ju came through the door. She was a vet at the zoo and, like Chen Cuiping, had been sent to work there after graduating from agricultural university. Her working hours usually coincided with Chang Jing's, but today she'd had to finish late because there was an antelope that had required minor surgery.

'Hey, where's your dad?' she called out in surprise.

Rocky hurriedly swallowed the food in his mouth and, shaking his head, said, 'He went out to buy cigarettes, but that was half an hour ago. I don't know where he's gone.'

'If you're hungry you can eat, just don't forget to leave him some pork.'

Rocky grunted and ran over to load up his bowl. He

suddenly remembered something, and turned back to say, 'When Baba left, he said we shouldn't wait for him and that we could just eat without him when you got back.'

'Well, that means he can't have gone to buy cigarettes...' Tong Ju replied. 'Where on earth could he be?'

'I bet he's gone to play mah-jong again.'

'I don't think so, not without eating his dinner. Besides, he wouldn't have the guts to do it even if he wanted to.'

'Mum, why are you always so mean to Dad? He's much stronger than you, you know.'

'So what if he's strong? As if he'd dare lay a finger on me! He might spend his day bossing tigers around, but he rolls over as soon as he sees me.'

'Does that mean you're scarier than a tiger, Mum?'

'Of course. Now eat your dinner.'

By now, Tong Ju had taken off her coat and spooned some of the food into her bowl. An air of expectancy hung over the table, and their dinner seemed to take a little longer to finish than normal. Twice during the meal did Tong Ju lay down her chopsticks to open the door and see who was coming up the stairs. Anger simmered inside of her; were Chang Jing to walk through the door that instant, he would have been hit with a torrent of abuse. Yet he had still not returned by the time they finished eating, so Tong Ju went over and locked the front door.

She was too furious to do the washing up, and just left everything on the dining table and went straight to bed with Rocky. Once tucked under the quilt, Rocky said, 'Mum, I know where Baba went.'

'Where?' she asked.

'I think he might have gone to beat up Li Dabing.'

'I doubt that – he's scared of Li Dabing more than anyone else. Even if he had a pair, he wouldn't go and fight him.'

'You shouldn't say that about Dad. Even the tigers do as he says, so Li Dabing is nothing.'

'Those tigers are tame – Li Dabing is a whole different kettle of fish.'

'Well, it doesn't matter what you think. I know Dad's gone round to duff Dabing up, just like I did to Li Chao today.'

'OK, it sounds to me like I'm not getting the whole story here. I want you to get up and tell me what happened earlier,' Tong Ju said, dragging Rocky out from under the blanket. He curled up into a ball, giggling. 'What are you doing, Mum?'

But Tong Ju had a face like thunder. 'What the hell is going on? Why would your dad go fight Li Dabing?'

'Maybe cos of what I said to him this afternoon.'

'What did you say that would make him want to start a fight?'

'I didn't say anything actually,' Rocky replied. 'I was gonna say something, but then I didn't. I just hmphed and walked away.'

'You hmphed at your father? You're old enough now to have more manners than that. And what's this about *you* getting into a fight? What did Li Chao do to provoke you?'

'He didn't provoke me, it was his dad. I went to the zoo during lunch break to get my meal voucher from Dad, but I couldn't find him anywhere. Then I bumped into Chen Juanmao from the monkey enclosure, and he said Dad was in the office building. So I went there, and finally I found him. He was standing in front of stupid Li Dabing's desk, and Dabing had this really weird look on his face. I couldn't hear what he was saying through the glass, but I knew it wasn't anything nice. And Baba was just standing there, like a cat being told off by a mouse. Eventually, he noticed me through the window, and I just hmphed and ran away. During afternoon break, I went over to Li Chao and got revenge.'

Tong Ju waited for Rocky to finish, and said, 'Well, aren't you growing up fast? Messing around in grown-ups' business already.'

'You're not gonna make me kneel on the washboard[1] are you?' Rocky said.

Tong Ju sat down on the bed, her face ashen. Rocky took one look at her and got up, put his clothes back on, fetched the washboard and knelt down on it. His mother stood up, skirted around him and went out the front door without saying a word.

3

Rocky stayed kneeling on the washboard for a minute or so, but when he heard no sound of movement coming from outside, he got up and left the flat, descending the stairs until he reached the road that ran through the village.

Half-walking, half-running, it didn't take him long to see the silhouette of his mother up ahead. Just as he'd suspected, she was heading in the direction of Li Dabing's house. Rocky regretted having said anything; he'd initially decided it would be best not to tell her where his dad had gone, which is why he didn't say anything over dinner. But then it had grown late and his dad still hadn't come back, so he'd started to worry and ended up telling her everything.

Rocky hadn't expected his father to be so easily goaded into action. But deep down, he was pleased with his little ruse and his father's reaction to it. Because he hadn't actually heard Li Chao talking about Chang Jing owing their family a life; that rumour had been flying around the zoo for years and Rocky had first heard it ages ago. The reason he wanted to stir things up today was so that his father knew that two generations of the Li family had insulted them. Rocky had already defended the Chang family honour with his fists, and now he wanted his father to do the same.

Rocky padded after his mother as silently as a cat, keeping ten paces between them. Three or four minutes later, they were approaching Li Dabing's apartment building when a rabble spilled out of the main entrance. Rocky hid behind a streetlamp and watched his mother as she strode into the shadowy crowd. He heard his father's voice, then the sound of his mother arguing with someone.

'Why are you arresting my husband? Let him go!'

Hearing this, Rocky darted out from his hiding place. Slowly making their way through the crowd of people were two uniformed police officers, with his baba in between them. Off to one side, he could see the Li family. His mum was blocking the way, hands on her hips, attempting to rescue his father like a female Robin Hood.

Her valour did not receive the attention it deserved, however. The policemen didn't even deign speak to her, simply angling their shoulders so they could walk past.

Rocky felt himself flooded with a sense of youthful heroism. He became a fierce tiger cub, blocking the way like his mother had with his hands on his hips, and roared, 'Li Chao, you better tell your dad to let my dad go!'

As the crowd stared blankly, he shot off like an arrow, grabbing Li Chao by the wrist and dragging him underneath a lamp post a few metres away.

'If you don't let my dad go, I'm gonna bash his head in!' Rocky shouted in the glow of the streetlamp. His left arm had a tight grip on Li Chao, who was half a head shorter than him, while his right hand held up half of a mud-covered brick.

Rocky did his best to look convincing, as though he would actually go through with it if nobody stopped him. The threat had its desired effect.

The two police officers walked over to him and in coaxing voices said, 'Hey there buddy, now you don't want to do that, do you? We're not arresting your dad, we just want to talk to him.'

'No,' Rocky retorted. 'I want him to come home right now.'

In reality, Rocky had absolutely no intention of hurting Li Chao, because he knew that if he did, he would never be able to save his father. The threat was only effective so long as it wasn't actually carried out. If that brick came crashing down, he'd have no cards left to play.

Rocky faced off against the police officers while Li Chao sobbed loudly in fear. The spectators, meanwhile, had automatically retreated to the sidelines so they could get a good view of how the drama was going to play out.

After a minute or so, Li Dabing capitulated and said, 'Officers, I think it would be best if our two families settled this matter privately. Don't you agree?'

Police officer A glanced at police officer B, and both nodded in agreement; they obviously weren't too keen on getting involved in a domestic squabble.

And that was the end of that. Rocky tossed away the brick, shoved Li Chao to one side, and ran over to rejoin his parents as they walked back home.

4

Zoos are peculiar places, where animals are the stars and the humans all work backstage. And whenever somewhere has more animals than humans, the humans tend to feel isolated. The upshot of this was that any piece of gossip would spread through the zoo like an infectious disease, as the workers desperately clawed for anything they could use to stave off their loneliness.

News of what happened that night between Chang and Li began to spread the very next day. The general consensus was that Rocky was a force to be reckoned with; everyone who crossed paths with Chang Jing would say, 'That's some kid you've got there!' He was secretly very happy to hear this, of course, but out loud he'd say, 'Oh, that boy is forever getting himself in trouble.'

It didn't take long for Rocky to also catch wind of what everyone was saying about him. He was proud of himself, and it gave him a new idea. A few days later, he plotted a trap to bury Li Chao in the school's sandpit, usually used for practising long jump.

One day after school, Rocky waited for Li Chao to come out of class and went over to him with an air of reconciliation. He gave Li Chao a sleek metal catapult, and sincerely apologised for what had happened between them. The two boys then found a quiet spot where they could sit down and have a long heart-to-heart.

But Rocky wasn't really interested in making friends with Li Chao. He was simply waiting for it to get dark.

When the moon finally made its appearance, a savage expression transformed Rocky's face. He pulled a length of rope out of his bag and forcibly trussed Li Chao up like a *zongzi*.[2] Li Chao began to shout for help, but Rocky's threats soon shut the smaller boy up. Rocky then proceeded to bury Li Chao up to his neck in the sandpit.

'I can hardly breathe!' Li Chao cried.

'You deserve it. And who taught you to be so greedy? Did you really think I'd just give you this catapult?' taunted Rocky, brandishing it in Li Chao's face. 'Idiot.'

'Please let me go.'

'Sure I'll let you go, but you've gotta answer my questions first.'

'OK.'

'You've heard that my family owes your family a life, right?'

'Yeah.'

'Who did you hear it from? Was it your dad?'

'No. People at the zoo.'

'Who?'

'I don't remember.'

'And what do they say, exactly?'

'I really can't breathe, Rocky. Can't you take off some of the sand?'

Rocky could tell from Li Chao's little face that he was indeed struggling, so he kicked away some of the sand from around his chest. 'OK, now I want you to tell me everything.'

'They say that my dad had a twin brother who was eaten by a tiger at the zoo. Your dad was the only one there when it happened, because my dad had gone off for a wee in the bushes, and while he was gone my uncle fell into the river around the tiger enclosure. My dad came running back and saw the tiger dragging his brother into its cave. Everyone says it was your dad who accidentally knocked my uncle into the enclosure, and so your family owes my family a life.'

'And do you believe that?' Rocky asked.

'I don't know, it happened before I was born.'

Satisfied with this answer, Rocky heaved Li Chao out from the sandpit and went to hang off a nearby set of monkey bars. 'And now let me tell you, my dad had nothing to do with your uncle getting eaten. When the three of them were hanging out in the zoo that time, there was someone else there too: your mum. She saw with her own eyes that your uncle was next to the rail one minute, and the next he'd disappeared. She was so scared.'

Li Chao said, 'You weren't born then either, so how do you know all this? You're making it sound like you were there.'

'I heard my dad talking about it. He hates your mum, because she saw everything but never stuck up for him.'

'Why are you telling me all this?' Li Chao asked.

'I just wanted to tell you that your uncle's death had nothing to do with my family. Him falling in was just an accident, so our family doesn't owe your family a life. Our family doesn't owe your family anything, actually. That's what I want you to remember. Also, don't forget that the tiger that ate your uncle was a Bengal tiger. Do you know what a Bengal tiger is? It's the type of tiger that my dad trains. And if you dare say anything to your parents about what happened today, I'll make sure it eats you too.'

5

Rocky went straight home after untying Li Chao, oblivious to the thought that he might get into serious trouble for his actions. That same night, Li Chao fell ill. He had a burning fever, his eyes were glazed over, and he kept on screaming, 'Don't eat me, Rocky! Don't eat me!' When his parents asked him what was wrong, he just stared back at them blankly as though possessed by a ghost.

When Li Dabing and his wife came to lay blame at the Chang family's door, their eyes were visibly swollen from crying – the doctor had told them that their child was probably broken. What did that mean, 'broken'? It meant that something had snapped in Li Chao's brain and it probably wouldn't be possible to fix it. To his parents, it felt like they had lost their son.

Arguing was futile by this point, and after a series of heated altercations, both families finally decided to sit down and discuss matters calmly.

Throughout this entire time, Rocky was on the receiving end of frequent beatings at home. On one occasion, Chang Jing spanked him with a shoe so hard that the sole split. The outcome of the negotiations was that Chen Cuiping would take time off work so she could take Li Chao to see a specialist in Beijing. The Changs would initially give her ¥20,000 to cover her lost wages and medical expenses, and if that didn't turn out to be enough, they would cover up to ¥50,000. In the event that Li Chao's condition was deemed incurable, the Changs would pay ¥100,000 in damages to cover his future living expenses.

The night this agreement was reached, Chang Jing spanked Rocky so ferociously with his shoe that he drew blood. Rocky's piercing cries seemed to fill every corner of Zoo Village. Yet this punishment was justified because the amount of money Chang Jing and Tong Ju were going to have to pay out was the equivalent of ten years' wages.

It's here that the story takes a turn, one that nobody was expecting but one that nobody was surprised by. Two weeks after these events took place, Chang Jing and his family moved out of Zoo Village. Before leaving, they secretly sold off their flat and any belongings they couldn't take with them. No one knew where they went, which was exactly how they wanted it.

6

Li Dabing phoned his wife in Beijing to tell her about the Changs' disappearance, and to ask how their son was recovering. Chen Cuiping reported that Li Chao's condition was under control, but the doctors didn't know if there were going to be any long-term repercussions. She didn't have anything to say about the Chang family. She hung up.

Chen Cuiping sat in her chair and listened to her heartbeat, rapid and surging, as she drifted down a river of old memories.

She saw a pretty university student lying in the shade in a remote corner of the zoo, surrounded by a gentle rustling of leaves and occasional snorts from the distant animals. A tall, strapping young man was staring down at her adoringly, then slowly leant over her. She smiled shyly and closed her eyes.

But five minutes later, she'd regretted it. She was in tears, the young man talking non-stop in an effort to console her. They soon got up and returned to the footpath, where they almost instantly came across a short, bespectacled man; he'd been searching high and low for them, but he was five minutes too late. Little did any of them know how much difference those five minutes were going to make.

Notes

1. A typical form of punishment, usually doled out by wives to their husbands.
2. A traditional Chinese rice dish made of glutinous rice stuffed with different fillings and wrapped in bamboo leaves, or sometimes, with reed leaves, or other large flat leaves, then steamed or boiled.

Woman Dancing under Stars

Teng Xiaolan

Translated by Yu Yan Chen

On my way home from work, I stopped by 85°C Bakery for some bread. An elderly, grey-haired woman stood in front of me in the queue; she didn't order anything except for a cup of wheat milk tea. As the cashier placed the tea in her hands, she spoke in a crisp, standard Shanghainese:

'Excuse me, do you mind giving me two more packets of white sugar, please?'

The cashier paused. 'The cup's been sealed. We won't be able to add it now, I'm afraid.'

'No problem, I can do it myself,' she replied calmly, 'The other young lady gave it to me last time. Thank you.'

Holding her tea and sugar, the old woman shuffled to a nearby window seat and sat down. Carefully taking off the plastic seal, she poured in the sugar, stirred it, took a sip and began reading her newspaper.

As I was leaving, her newspaper fell on the floor, so I picked it up and gave it back to her.

'Thanks so much,' she smiled at me.

I grinned back. She seemed to be in her seventies but looked good for her age. There were no wrinkles on her face and her skin was fair. She sported a cream-coloured turtleneck sweater with a plaid jacket. A diamond ring glistened on her finger.

Several days later, I ran into the woman there again. She was sitting at the same window seat reading her newspaper. The afternoon sun shone on the table, as warm as a cup of newly-brewed milk tea. The queue was extremely long, so I sat down to wait.

The old woman raised her head and her eyes met mine. 'Oh, it's you again, *meimei*,'[1] she said.

'Hello,' I offered.

We chatted casually for a few minutes when suddenly she blurted out, 'Are you a newlywed?'

'How do you know?' I was slightly surprised.

'Your fragrance; there's a sweetness to it that belongs exclusively to newlyweds. It's difficult not to notice it.'

I couldn't help but turn red – it's very rare to find a woman of her age speaking in such a frank manner – but I told her that I got married in the beginning of that month. 'You're still on your honeymoon!' she said, and I blushed.

Her name was Zhuge Wei. Out of respect, I normally never ask older people for their names, but she volunteered it, and before I knew it she had invited me to her house. '*Meimei*,' she confided, 'I think we get along splendidly.'

Who knew if we would get along – we'd barely exchanged a few sentences. So I declined the invitation tactfully: 'I already have plans, let's do it some other time…'

She seemed disappointed. 'In that case, yes, let's do it another time.'

As soon as I got home, I followed the cookbook instructions and fixed dinner in a hurry. Instead of minced, the pork was chunkier – more suitable for braising than mixing with a spicy sauce. Then there was too little water for the rice, so it wasn't fully cooked. I'd forgotten to descale the fillets in the fish and spring onion dish. As usual, my husband showered me with praise. 'I've never eaten anything tastier!' Such is lovers' talk when still in this honeymoon phase. How on earth could he enjoy food like this?

'What a messy meal!' I lamented.

'But a delicious messiness!' he replied.

I suddenly recalled what Ms Zhuge said and told my husband about our chance encounter.

'Having a cup of milk tea alone?' My husband was taken aback. 'What a weirdo!'

'Why can't an old woman have a cup of milk tea on her own?' I rebutted. 'When I am old, maybe I'll do that too.'

'You won't,' said my husband. 'I'll be there with you. We'll be an old couple having tea together.'

Ms Zhuge's husband was probably no longer with us. My husband had a point: a woman of her age having a cup of milk tea all on her own was indeed slightly unusual round here. I suspected that she didn't have any grandchildren either. Senior citizens with grandchildren would definitely have no time for tea.

Less than two days later, I ran into her again at the supermarket. She was choosing a steak and when she spotted me, she asked for help. 'Which one is better, the one from Australia or the one from Japan?' I glanced at the prices and the one from Japan seemed more expensive, so I advised her to take the one from Australia, given that both looked more or less the same. Ms Zhuge took the steak and picked out a bottle of red wine.

'*Meimei*, would you like to have dinner with me tonight? I only live round the corner.'

My husband happened to be on a business trip that day, so I accepted her invitation. I was only going to grab something quick for dinner anyway. Although I didn't want to trouble others, Ms Zhuge looked sincere. Not to mention, at 5'5" I felt quite secure dining with an old lady less than 5'2" in height.

'That sounds fine, *Ah Po*.'[2] I blurted out the expression without knowing whether she liked it or not. As an old lady who dines on steak with red wine, maybe it would be better for me to address her as 'Ms' or 'Miss'?

I noticed that she paid with a credit card at the cash register and that her signature was very elegant. She'd also brought her own shopping bag, into which the steak and red wine disappeared. 'Let's go, my dear.' As she spoke, she wanted to hold my hand, but missed when I shrunk back. Feeling embarrassed, I grabbed one of her arms instead. It made me laugh to be so intimate with a stranger; I could smell her perfume, along with a faint scent of soap.

Soon we arrived at her house, a building not too far from mine. There were only two buildings in this cluster, with lots of trees and well-managed gardens. She lived in the building nearer the road, in a loft with three bedrooms and two living rooms. As she showed me around the flat, I noticed how quaint most of the decor was, with all its vintage colours. Several pieces of her furniture were made of redwood and the displays on the shelves were mostly antiques, including the Four Treasures of the Study – brush, inkstick, paper and ink stone – as well as other pieces inlaid with gold and jade. The one item that stood out was a wooden dancing lady, who wore an elegant dress that extended all the way to the floor. The background was also made of wood, engraved to look like a vivid starry night. Both the figurine and the background stood on the same board. There was even a rooftop patio on the upper level of Ms Zhuge's flat, which had been converted into a sun lounge full of plants, like a little garden.

Before going to the kitchen to prepare the food, she told me to relax and make myself at home. I sat on the sofa and looked around. There were no family portraits and only a few pieces of women's clothing left drying on the patio. No trace of any children, and I was sure she was the flat's only resident.

The steak was cooked to the right tenderness, and the red

wine was a 2004 Cabernet Sauvignon from Chile. There was a nice fragrance with the first sip and when I swirled it, there were enough wine legs on the side of the glass as well.

Ms Zhuge asked me, 'How old are you?'

'Twenty-nine,' I replied.

She hummed curiously, and commented, 'You married quite late then.'

I smiled and ruminated on what to do to repay her. The Australian steak wasn't cheap and there was the red wine on top of it. Since we had only just met, of course I didn't consider inviting her to my place, but the idea of getting a free meal out of her didn't sit well with me either.

'Ah Po,' I said, 'are you free this weekend? Would you like to grab a drink at Starbucks?'

Delighted, she accepted my invitation.

Before we parted, she invited me up to the patio. The night was getting chilly, so I wrapped my jacket around me as we sat together on the wicker chairs. Above us shone a blanket of stars, each twinkling so brilliantly that it was as though we could reach out and touch them. It was the first time since I'd moved to the city that I'd savoured such a beautiful night, and the fragrance of the flowers and greenery around me only deepened how content I felt.

'Do you sit like this often and watch the stars?' I asked.

She seemed to be deep in thought, with her head raised, and didn't even blink her eyes. My question didn't appear to register until much later, when she suddenly asked, 'Do you see the stars dancing?'

I hesitated.

'Look, the stars are moving – they're dancing.' Her tone suggested nothing but seriousness, and I felt awkward. She stared at me and repeated her question, 'Do you see that they're dancing?'

All I could do was nod.

On my way back, I couldn't help but look at the sky. The stars were just like the ones on the patio. *Were* they dancing? I squinted and quickened my pace home.

Since I had to work on both Saturday and Sunday, I forgot about our appointment at Starbucks. By the time I remembered, it was Monday morning. I jerked fully awaked like a frightened rabbit with an 'Oh no!'

My husband thought I was making a mountain out of a molehill. 'You don't really know her, what's the big deal?'

When I got off work that day, I stopped by the 85°C Bakery especially to look for Ms Zhuge, but I didn't see her. This made me feel a bit lost. How embarrassing – I didn't even keep an appointment with an old lady. She probably now thinks of me as an untrustworthy woman, just like any other impetuous youth making frivolous promises.

I sat down frustrated, then heard someone behind me calling, *'Meimei!'*

Turning around, I saw a beaming Ms Zhuge waving at me. I waved back, feeling much more uplifted. 'Hello, *Ah Po.*'

As I explained why I couldn't meet up with her over the weekend, she shook her hands. 'No problem, work is more important. The coffee at Starbucks isn't any good. American coffee is too weak. I like Manabe – Japanese coffee is much more refined.'

I said I would treat her at Manabe, but she declined. 'We're already here, why do we need to go to Manabe? The milk tea from Taiwan is very nice too.' I smiled and ordered two wheat milk teas and two pieces of cake at the counter. We looked for a table by the window and sat down.

This time we exchanged more personal details about ourselves. As I'd expected, Ms Zhuge's husband passed away more than a decade ago and they didn't have any children. 'My husband was an architect and he designed several famous buildings in this city. We were classmates in secondary school and got married after graduating from university. We had one child, but he passed away at the age of five.' She spoke so calmly even when it came to the death of her child, it was like she was simply recounting the experiences of others.

To return the favour, I also briefly talked about myself. I graduated with a journalism degree and currently work as a reporter at a news agency, I explained. My husband and I used to attend the same university and we dated for eight years. We bought a house together at the end of last year and got married as soon as it was renovated.

'Are you ready to have children?' she asked.

'I'll go with the flow,' I said.

After chatting with Ms Zhuge for more than half an hour, I stood up to say goodbye. 'Leaving so soon,' she said. 'All right then, let's chat next time.' When I heard that, my initial response was to wonder how there could be a next time, but I smiled and said nothing. For a person who disliked starting conversations with strangers, the few encounters with Ms Zhuge had been exceptions. Soon, I presumed, we would retreat into our own worlds and never see each other again – like two straight lines, having crossed once, our paths unlikely to cross again.

One day, after cooking dinner every night for two months, I went a little crazy.

'What's the point in praising me repeatedly?' I ranted at my husband. 'I quit! If you can heap high praise on food like this, it can mean only one thing – you're a liar. You come home every day and expect dinner to be ready – do you see anything wrong with this picture? If I kept my mouth shut, do you think I'd carry on cooking for you for the rest of your life?'

My husband was astonished. Any other woman would have begun with some complaints first, before blowing her lid – gone through a transitional period, if you like – but not me.

I liked to bring things to a head, straightaway. One minute I'm a virtuous wife, the next I'm a screaming lioness. I endured the sole responsibility for the chores for exactly two months, no more and no less. Like a product made in Japan, I am perfect during the warranty period but as soon as it's over, the whole thing falls apart.

He still tried to pretend that nothing was wrong. Putting his arm around me, he began, 'Honey –'

I pushed it away. 'You'll be cooking dinner tomorrow, okay?'

He agreed. Then, with a knot in my throat, I cleared away the dishes and washed them in the kitchen. He came over with a cheeky smile and said that he would help me with the washing up. I declined.

'Whoever cooks that night will be responsible for the dishes – it'll be a one-stop-shop. Starting from tomorrow. We'll take turns cooking from Monday to Friday. This won't change unless a special occasion calls for it. If we're not going to our parents' houses at the weekend, then I will cook. If you agree, please sign your name on the affidavit over there.' I pointed at the A4 letter on the table.

My husband went over to the table, baffled. 'It's a shame. You should be working as a secretary-general at the state council, you get things done so efficiently,' he said as he signed the paper. After that, I snapped out of the bad mood and began to relax.

'Go watch some TV, I'll peel an apple for you later.'

He suggested going out for a late screening, but I declined because I had work the next day. After taking a shower and getting into bed, he made love to me. He was especially considerate that night, with an obvious intent to please. While I responded to it, I realised that men are much more thick-skinned. Our curtain was not fully closed, so a few stars slipped into the room, reaching us from so far away. Afterwards I thought of Ms Zhuge, the night we stargazed on her patio. It wasn't as cramped and the sky felt so close then, as though I was alone in the universe with stars right above my head. Only in that kind of environment can Ms Zhuge sense that the stars are dancing. She was all alone, without a husband or a child. Her heart was probably made of glass too, just like the sun lounge she'd created – what an exquisite old lady.

On the phone my husband said that he had to stop by the market to pick up ingredients for dinner, but he also fancied some garlic bread from the 85°C Bakery and asked me to get it.

As I entered the café, I saw Ms Zhuge sitting in front of the window reading her paper, forming a ninety-degree angle with the table. Shanghainese slang would have described it as 'showing great frame.' Indeed, she was very meticulous about her posture. I hid in the long queue and tried to avoid being spotted. The assistant packed and took payments at a leisurely pace, and the queue grew longer. Someone started to complain and the atmosphere soured. After I was finally able to pay, I walked directly to the door.

An old woman in a grey blouse pushed the door open and bumped right into me. Although I cried out irritably, she rushed to Ms Zhuge without stopping.

What happened next was like something from a movie.

She grabbed the tea on the table and poured it over Ms Zhuge. 'Old bitch!' she spat, her face contorted with rage.

It was so sudden and loud that everyone in the café froze in astonishment.

The tawny liquid dripped from Ms Zhuge's hair. She looked in disbelief at the woman standing in front of her, prompting the other woman to slap her with a loud, crisp smack.

'Old slut!'

Ms Zhuge stared daggers at the woman, but her voice

remained calm. 'Who are you?' she enquired.

Instead of replying, she spat, 'Old bitch, no wonder you have neither husband nor children.' What a hurtful curse.

Then an old man barged in. 'It must be bad karma from a previous life – you win, old woman,' he mumbled as he began to drag the woman in grey outside. She struggled in his grip, but her arm was firmly restrained by him in a painful-looking position. Somehow he managed to greet Ms Zhuge with his head lowered. 'I am so sorry about this, so sorry –'

The pair left the bakery quickly, leaving Ms Zhuge alone. The bystanders could somehow guess what the drama was about, but considering the ages of the parties involved, it came as a surprise. It looked like the old folk's version of 'wife catching the mistress.'

Ms Zhuge took out some napkins and wiped away the milk tea from her face. Some had got on her clothes, which she dabbed a wet-wipe at softly and meticulously, with all her usual elegance. Using a small comb from her bag, she made her slightly mussed hair neat again, the diamond ring on her finger twinkling as she did so. After a few minutes she got up, straightened out her clothes and left.

The bystanders in the café watched her go, then quickly returned to whatever they were doing. Although it had been an interesting afternoon development, it would soon be forgotten.

The shadows of the street lengthened as the afternoon sun descended in the west. I followed Ms Zhuge, who was trudging heavily along, but at a sufficient distance to not attract attention. Then she stopped by a big tree, leaning with an outstretched hand against its trunk. I stopped too and watched her.

She looked sad from the back. No one should have to put up with that kind of insult, especially not an old woman. I approached her, driven by an unknown force.

'How are you, *Ah Po*?' I tried my best to sound relaxed. 'What a coincidence, us meeting again.'

She turned and said, 'Hi.'

While I considered what to say to cheer her up, I suddenly caught sight of the 85°C Bakery bag in my hand and became tongue-tied, which Ms Zhuge quickly spotted. She laughed it off.

'That old lady is seven to eight years younger than me, but you can't tell, can you?'

I paused for a moment and suddenly understood what she really meant   the woman in the grey blouse showed her age because she didn't take as good care of herself as Ms Zhuge. But why was she bringing this up at such a moment? It was strange.

'That's true,' I agreed, 'she looked at least five years older than you.'

Ms Zhuge explained that the old man was her dance partner. They dance together at the square in front of Carrefour every night. 'We were simply exercising. Many old folks dance there, which is a good thing. I wonder what got into his wife – I was dumbfounded by what she said.' Ms Zhuge spoke slowly and didn't seem particularly angry about it, only a bit surprised.

'She was jealous.' I giggled.

Ms Zhuge sighed. 'It's a shame since we've developed a rapport after dancing together for so long. Mr Feng has good rhythm.'

They had registered for the city's senior citizen dance competition. 'That's impossible, now.' She couldn't help but sigh again.

I tried to comfort her. 'Go for the next competition if you can't make it this year. You can always get a new partner and start practising right away. You still have plenty of time.'

We continued strolling. 'Do you dance?' she asked.

I shook my head.

'Dancing is good for a woman,' she said. 'You become prettier while keeping fit.'

'How?' I couldn't imagine how the first part worked.

'When a man puts his hand on your shoulder…' she gestured, putting her hand on my shoulder, as though she was reciting poetry. 'Your body becomes light and soft, even pliant, and every move seems sexier, more elegant and graceful, because you will want to show your best face to him.'

I continued to smile but felt a bit disdainful. In fact, I almost began to sympathise with the old lady in the café earlier. How should I put it… what Ms Zhuge said made me feel awkward even though I was not yet thirty. She was the same age as my grandma. But aside from my grandpa's, Grandma has probably never put her hand on any man's shoulder. As for the woman who had made a scene, her hands seemed dark and coarse, and she had eye bags as deep as birds' nests. I could hardly contemplate the differences between the two women.

'She has a slutty spirit.' My husband later commented, on hearing the story. 'If her husband were still alive, he'd probably be furious.'

'Is it true that men like slutty women?' I asked jokingly.

My husband snorted in reply.

I repeated the question a week later – it wasn't a joke, but I pretended it was. My company had had a year-end party at a restaurant, and on my way to the toilet, I spotted my husband sitting at a table in the far corner with a rather slutty-looking woman. They looked very intimate. When I got back to my seat, I phoned him and asked where he was. He said that he was working overtime.

'Do men usually like slutty women?' I asked him while lying in bed, smiling like a virtuous wife.

Once again, he snorted in reply.

I hardly had any sleep that night and went to work the next morning without my breakfast. A headache bothered me the whole morning and by noon I couldn't stand it and asked my manager if I could leave. As soon as I arrived home, I sank into a stupor for the rest of the afternoon. Some time after five, I turned on my mobile and saw my husband's text: he wanted braised pork that night and asked if I could please make it.

I scowled, stomped out of the flat and ordered myself a set meal at a nearby restaurant. I ate at a snail's pace and continued to linger even when the nearby table had changed customers. A waitress with apple cheeks kept on staring at me like I was about to run away without paying. My phone was busy, vibrating with texts and phone calls. I ignored it completely.

When I finally left around 11pm, I wandered the streets. Except for the occasional cyclist, there were very few pedestrians. The streetlamps stretched my shadow into various lengths, as though I were a rubber band. I suddenly felt like a fool for meandering like this. Whatever needed to be said was left unsaid, whatever needed to be cursed was left uncursed. I was cutting off my nose to spite my face and it was simply stifling.

Human beings have a knack for the unexpected, especially when they're in a compromising situation. It's like getting drunk and involuntarily following your subconscious; mine was still lucid enough to know that I couldn't go back to my parents' house because they would worry, that of course I couldn't go to my in-laws because it would exasperate things rather than help, and that there were no friends I could turn to because everyone had a family. It would do no good except to make me feel embarrassed on top of everything else.

A few minutes later I found myself at the building where Ms Zhuge lived, ringing the bell. A moment passed and then a voice crackled through the intercom, 'Who is it?'

'It's me, *Ah Po*,' I replied.

Ms Zhuge was waiting for me at her door when I walked out of the elevator. She seemed pleasantly surprised. On a terrible night like this, seeing someone actually welcoming my arrival, I couldn't help but feel comforted by that warmth. Abruptly something burned in my nose and tears streamed down my cheeks before I could stop them. I covered my face with my hands. Ms Zhuge pulled me into her flat and made me a cup of pu'erh tea.[3]

'It's so cold outside,' she put the cup in my hands. 'Warm your hands first.'

I told her the problems I had with my husband. Since I showed up in the middle of the night, there was no way of hiding it. Ms Zhuge offered me some snacks. 'Have some.'

'*Ah Po*,' I said, 'I'm so sorry to bother you.'

'You're not a bother – you don't know how happy I am to see you,' she smiled.

As my hands gradually warmed, so did my heart, bit by bit. The aroma of the pu'erh tea rose and its steam gently licked my face.

Ms Zhuge asked, 'Do you love your husband very much?'

I considered for a moment and nodded my head, rather unwillingly.

After talking to her for a while longer, she tried to convince me to go home.

'I'm not chasing you out, *meimei*. My advice is to pretend you don't know anything when you get back and never bring it up again. Women and men are different. In order to hold on to something, sometimes you have to relax your grip. Tears should only be shed inside; you have to smile outside – smile brilliantly, that way you will be able to hold on to whatever you want till the end. Come on, think about it.'

I thought over her words. They sounded very simple but

had great depth to them. While I sat quietly, Ms Zhuge asked whether I wanted to learn how to dance. I hesitated and then agreed.

'In that case, go home first and come back Friday night. I will teach you then.'

My husband was watching TV in bed when I got home. He asked where I went because I didn't answer his call. I said it was on vibrate and I didn't hear it, that I had ran into an old classmate and we went to dinner together.

'What classmate,' he asked, 'male or female?'

'Male,' I purposely lied. He snorted once more. I recalled what Ms Zhuge said – if a woman wants to hold on to something, sometimes she has to relax. I took three deep breaths and swallowed the resentful words I was so tempted to say. I took a shower and saw my slightly bulging stomach in the mirror, along with a few fine lines under my eyes.

Before going to bed, I did 50 sit-ups and put on a collagen face mask. Each one costs over a hundred RMB. I had been saving it for so long that it had nearly expired. My husband watched me, at first quietly, and then he commented snidely, 'You seem really worked up after seeing that male classmate.'

That weekend Ms Zhuge taught me how to dance rumba. She said rumba would be the most appropriate for someone like me, who sits in an office all day and often has lower back and neck issues. We tried a few basic moves together and she praised me for having a good sense of the movements. She asked me to relax my whole body, along with my mood.

'Don't think of anything. Just focus on dancing itself. Think of yourself as the most beautiful girl in the world, no one is as pretty as you.'

Her voice had a hypnotic effect on me. I let go of all my thoughts – only music could touch me while my feet moved, full of confidence. Ms Zhuge was a good teacher. She was patient and diligent, showing me the steps repeatedly until I got them. In fact, I knew exactly how terrible I was when it came to dancing. When I was in university, I tried to learn it many times but never succeeded because my body was as stiff as iron. This stiffness, I think, was reflected elsewhere in my life: my husband often complained that I wasn't feminine enough. For instance, I am very straightforward and even the way I dress can be a little uninspiring. The same could be said when it came to sex – once it starts, we both know how it will end, it is so lacking in variation.

Ms Zhuge found a new dance partner for herself shortly afterwards, a gentleman in his 60s from Ningbo. Every night she'd dance away with him in the square, and one night I went there just to watch. The sound of music permeated the surrounding area. It was my first time seeing so many old folks dancing in each other's arms. Most of them lacked elegance, their waistlines too thick and their arms too stiff, their rhythm sometimes off, but by their sincere expressions I could tell that they were genuinely enjoying it. As Ms Zhuge mentioned, everyone seemed to feel at their best, regardless of gender, height, or job. As a result, they were transformed into a brilliant life force the moment they stepped onto the dance floor. I'd passed by many times in the past, but never once had I stopped to take a closer look. This really was a place of miracles.

Late one evening, after drinking a whole bottle of the Chilean Cabernet Sauvignon with Ms Zhuge, I went to her patio and sat down in the wicker chair, admiring the starry sky above. It was so splendid yet not in the least daunting, I realised. Beautiful things don't necessarily have to be cold. My approachable and lovely starry night! Like mischievous children, the stars above winked at me every so often. The sky seemed to flow like black silk, revealing its fine texture. I was mesmerised by it.

Ms Zhuge suggested that we dance together. Thus, on the

patio of her rooftop flat, the two women – one old and one young – began to dance together while counting the steps. One song led to another. Although I kept stepping on her toes and apologising repeatedly for it, my smile shone ever so brightly as time went by. On a night like this happiness seemed to rise from within, almost to the point of overflowing. It was something I'd never experienced before.

'Look,' Ms Zhuge said, 'the stars are dancing.'

I looked up – the stars were indeed moving. Not only that, they seemed to have a certain rhythm. Going forward, then back, forward, and back, whirling around – they were really dancing. I squinted and put my hand on the pergola, hoping to see it more clearly.

'You're looking at the stars, not the sun,' Ms Zhuge said to me jokingly.

I lied to my husband that I went to Hangzhou for a short trip with several classmates and slept at Ms Zhuge's flat that night. Although he sounded suspicious over the phone, I put down the phone immediately after saying goodbye.

Ms Zhuge showed me photographs taken long ago – some of her and her husband, others of her son when he was three years old. Her husband was a handsome man with a clean look; one could sense he was an intellectual just by looking at him. Her son had chubby cheeks and looked like the character Hao Shaowen in the film *Oolong Courtyard*. He was cute.

'Do you miss them?' I asked out of nowhere. The alcohol had made me bold.

Ms Zhuge didn't reply. After a long silence, she said, 'It was such a long time ago…'

'Why didn't you have another child?' I asked.

She responded with a smile, 'Even if we had, the first one would never be able to come back.'

I felt that something was amiss in that sentence, but I couldn't think of any quick reply. Soon drowsiness came over me, and I fell asleep. I dreamed that I was still dancing, this time in an unknown place. I couldn't make out the details, it was blurry at first, but gradually some light crept in and the sky was stitched with stars – I was dancing under the starry night.

'Meimei,' I heard someone talking to me in my dream. It was Ms Zhuge, her voice gentle and kind as she said, 'You dance so well, it's beautiful.'

I kept on smiling and danced as though I'd gone mad. Nothing could have stopped me from whirling around.

Before I left the next day, Ms Zhuge gave me the wooden carving with the dancing woman.

'It's called "Woman Dancing under Stars". I bought it several years ago in Hong Kong. *Meimei,* I want to give it to you because I have always felt that we get along splendidly,' she said.

After we parted, I was sent to Guangzhou for a business assignment for six months. When I came back to Shanghai, Ms Zhuge seemed to have moved. No one answered when I rang her bell. I couldn't find her drinking milk tea at the 85°C Bakery. When I asked the assistant about it, she said Ms Zhuge hadn't shown up for a while.

I felt somewhat lost at first, but quickly put it behind me. After all, we weren't connected by blood – whatever small impression she'd made on my life would inevitably be worn away by time.

Soon I got pregnant and gave birth to a baby girl. She inherited the good traits of my husband and I, and is quite the cutie pie. I went back to work after maternity leave; luckily the old position was still available and everything went smoothly as a result. My husband's job was going well and he became the director of the credit department where he worked, which was no small feat at his age.

When my daughter turned one we moved to our new home. We'd sold the old flat for the first down payment on the new flat, then borrowed another half-million yuan in a housing loan. We could feel some pressure from the monthly mortgage, but it was bearable. Since we bought it right before the huge price rise, we felt especially lucky, as though we'd had a windfall. The renovation was done by one of my designer friends. She really put her mind to it, especially in terms of using light to enhance the atmosphere. We had a house tour for relatives from both sides of our family and everyone said that it was great. To be able to afford a place in Shanghai on our own at our age is definitely an achievement – we're the envy of everyone, it has to be said.

When my daughter turned three, my paternal grandmother, who had always lived in the suburbs of Shanghai, passed away and was buried at the Pine and Crane Cemetery in Jiading. Our whole family went there on the day of the funeral. I carried my daughter and bowed three times in front of her grave. She took care of me when I was little, and I was fond of playing with her double chin while curled up in her embrace. She looked plumper in her photo, happy and content. Her photo lay side by side with my grandpa's, who passed away a long time ago. Grandma's name used to be written in red on the tombstone – now it had been traced over with black ink.[4]

My husband examined the nearby tombstones with enthusiasm. Whenever he saw strange names such as 'Number Three,' or 'Little Boy,' he would point them out to me. My mother tugged at the corner of my clothes, asking why my husband still acts like a child, and I smiled.

Suddenly, the name 'Zhuge Wei' on the tombstone one row ahead caught my eye. I froze initially but couldn't help but walk closer. It was her, I could tell from the photo. She had been buried with her husband and son, a family of three. Her husband's surname was Su; he was in his 50s in his photo.

Compared to Ms Zhuge's, he looked a lot younger. I looked at the dates engraved on the tomb. She'd passed away two years ago.

A young woman stood in front of her tomb, holding a bunch of flowers. She looked a bit like Ms Zhuge. I hesitated initially but then went up to her to say hi, and introduced myself as Ms Zhuge's neighbour. The young lady had a suspicious look on her face at first, so I mentioned that Ms Zhuge used to love milk tea, and the wooden figurine of 'Woman Dancing under Stars'. She finally believed me and revealed that she was Ms Zhuge's grandniece.

'How did Ms Zhuge pass?' I asked delicately.

She said it was due to colon cancer, which had dragged on for seven to eight years.

I was surprised at first, then shook my head and sighed. Recalling the days we spent together, I felt sad. Judging from the way she looked, who would have thought that she was sick? She was so open-minded and looked as pretty as a fairy when she danced. She mentioned over and over again how well we got along. What a lovely old lady, yet she had returned to the dust forever.

My husband was nearby, having fun playing with our daughter and promising her we'd go to McDonald's for lunch. She was so excited that her face shone. I wanted to warn him that our family might have plans for later, but I didn't. Let them think whatever they like.

Once again, I looked at Ms Zhuge's tombstone and a sadness came over me — if it weren't for her, perhaps my husband might not be with me right now, let alone our daughter. She was right, one must relax in order to hold on to whatever one wants. Initially I had to endure the pain, but gradually things got easier. In fact, my husband had mentioned that one of his female clients had expressed interest in him. 'She dressed sluttily and I found her off-putting from the very start…' I had no idea whether she was the same person at the restaurant all those years ago, but so much time had gone by that I didn't feel like digging deeper. I chose to think of it as my husband's confession and felt even more relieved.

Nowadays I go for yoga once a week and a beauty treatment twice a month. I look even younger than two years ago. My tummy is as flat as a teenage girl's and my skin is fair and well-moisturised. On sunny afternoons I would have a cup of coffee by myself at Starbucks, Manabe, or the 85°C Bakery. I dance occasionally, too, alone on the balcony on starry nights. Whenever I do that, I tell myself that nothing is important except myself. I am something worthy of cherishing.

Walking to the back of the tombstone, I saw a line engraved in small characters:

'I love this man and this child deeply. For their sake, I choose to continue living more carefree and beautifully.'

On our coach ride back, my daughter lay in the arms of my husband while he leaned on my shoulder, both of them asleep.

I leaned against the window. The sun was beating down and it made me drowsy. Soon, I too fell asleep and had a dream. I dreamed of a woman dancing under the stars. I couldn't see her face clearly, but her slender figure was clad in a long dress. Her movements were so elegant that there was an ethereal charm to them. Her toes kept on spinning on the ground, one circle after another, spinning.

Notes

1. *Meimei* is the typical Shanghainese way of addressing young women.

2. *Ah Po* is a Shanghainese term of endearment meaning 'Granny'.

3. A variety of fermented tea that stems from the Yunnan province of China, most commonly made from the large leaf (Assamica) variety of the Camellia Sinensis tea plant.

4. In China, it is customary for married couples to purchase a joint grave when the first person dies and to add the name of still-living widow (or widower) in red ink on the tombstone, alongside the deceased's name in black ink. Upon their death, the name of the widow (or widower) is changed to black.

The Novelist in the Attic

Shen Dacheng

Translated by Jack Hargreaves

BEFORE THE FIRST SIGNS of dusk show in the sky, the editors start to call it a day, stacking the pages of their half-finished manuscripts and clicking off the green-lampshaded lights above their desks. Offices fall dark one by one. The corridors connecting these offices clear a floor at a time. At his usual hour, the security guard appears – this house of culture promises no shocks, no surprises, nothing to fear – and by the time he has completed one lackadaisical patrol of the building, leaving a single lamp lit on every floor, the sky outside is pitch black. The small building that houses the publisher has fallen absolutely still. This is when the novelist chooses to step out of his room.

Through the attic door, he descends, down a flight of black marble stairs, around the landing corner and down another flight to the floor below. He strolls leisurely along the deserted corridor, under old fashioned chandeliers hung from exquisitely carved ceiling panels; past one office door, after another – all shut. At the end of the corridor, he stops. Fourteen tall, slender windows, set side by side, occupy more than half the wall before him. Through them he can see the line of wutong trees planted along the roadside. From spring to autumn, their green proliferates, steadily deepens, then just as steadily wanes; in winter only spindly, skeletal branches remain. When the leaves burgeon again into shady luxuriance, he can be found at these windows, watching for hours as the leaves sway here and there with every slight breeze, a dizzying spell that sets his head rolling as if aboard a ship sailing over verdure waves. This winter evening, however, windless, waveless, serene, he looks out onto the stark-naked treetop that is almost level with him. Then he continues down the staircase, stopping at each floor to wander aimlessly, before lingering briefly at each corridor's end to look afresh at the window-framed scenery: the wutong treetop; upper branches; lower branches; the broad trunk descending all the way to the ground. Finally he comes to the ground floor where the on-duty guard has just finished a patrol and is sat behind his walnut counter, ready to idle away his tedious empty hours, flicking through a newspaper, drinking tea, sitting until sometime between eight and nine when he will perform the final patrol, then retire to the off-duty lounge and not emerge again until his next shift.

The security guard has been listening to the sole remaining footsteps in the publishing house since their steady pad began far above him, resounding through every inch of the building. Decades ago, when the guard was still young and new to the job, he had felt compelled to exchange words with the novelist, if only to ascertain how many lines he had written that day. As time passed, to simply see the novelist's expression was enough. And now, with years of experience, he only need hear his footsteps. Having written plenty, the novelist, satisfied with himself, walks slowly; having written little, encumbered by distress, he walks slower still; either way it's slow, but the security guard has learnt to tell the difference. 'Today's been productive.' He makes his first assessment based on the sound of the footsteps alone. Then, seeing the novelist stride down the final flight of stairs, he expands: 'He's been on a roll recently, the writing is clearly going smoothly.' Beside the former director, the security guard is the person who understands the novelist best, a fact which has escaped the notice of all three.

The two share a brief greeting. Then the novelist, stopping in the building threshold, fastens the collar of his old overcoat, pushes open the door, steps outside and walks into the small, alluring avenue on which the publishing house stands. Passing the wutong tree that he has already contemplated from three tiers of perspective – high, middle, low – he now adopts a pedestrian's point of view to contemplate the tree once more. After all, a novelist should look at any one thing from every possible angle and, more importantly, never weary of doing so. He has ventured out to eat dinner. After dinner, he will take a long walk, then return to the publishing house, to his attic. The novelist lives in the publishing house, permanently.

Many years ago, the novelist requested an office from the publisher. Previously, he had published his debut novel with the press – a bestseller as it turned out. Before that, no one had thought anything of the book, nor much of him. His presiding editor had treated him with intense indifference; there was no shortage of writers like him, so no reason for high hopes.

But the book enjoyed a good run of luck. After selling steadily for over six months, by pure coincidence, an issue it addressed became a hot topic, a big social talking point, catapulting the work into the public consciousness. Copies flew off the shelves, stocks were cleared out, and after a swift reprinting, another swiftly followed. The novelist accepted invitations to several readings and Q&As, during which he presented the audience with a sufficiently fleeting impression of himself that none could ascertain whether they liked him or not. But that wasn't in the slightest bit important, because before long, film rights for the book were sold. Third-rate filmmakers, it seemed, recognised a greater talent in him than the novelist himself. The resulting movie was mediocre at best, yet still sparked a new wave of sales that launched the novelist into the upper echelons of bestselling author lists. Eager to capitalise on the momentum, the novelist released a second book which sold a seventh as well as the first. Not good enough, but passable. Then, partway through his third book, he asked the director to assign him a temporary space for writing in. The director wasn't a stickler for regulation and liked making friends. Right then, the novelist fitted the bill for friendship perfectly. They had discussed how once the new book was complete, his three works should be marketed as a set – a trilogy – to better draw eyes, win prizes and, ultimately, sell, never mind that there was no explicit link between the three – a shrewdly-chosen series title would fix that. The novelist put forth the quite innovative suggestion too that the cost for renting the space be deducted from the agreed upon fee for the new book. The director approved.

'Writing in-house can only be good for you.' The director reeled off the names of eight well-known writers from the previous generation, '…they all did it. It used to be the norm that writers were good friends with their publishers, their relationship transcended a business transaction, authors would be continually in touch with their editors; they'd go on walks together, share ideas, exchange advice and together produce great books.'

'Is that right?' replied the novelist. He wasn't in the mood to discuss companionship, he only wanted to explain his intention for renting the space, 'I'll come at nine in the morning and leave at five, there's nothing to disturb me here, and I'll have a writing routine. I want to give this life a try.'

The director approved, 'Well, it can only be a good thing. There's no other way to write a book as far as I'm concerned. You have to write one hundred characters a hundred times to have ten thousand characters, and write ten thousand characters twenty times to have the two hundred thousand characters to make a book. There should be no talk of two hundred thousand characters' worth of talent, only two hundred thousand characters of effective work. A writer must exert themselves.'

'Exactly,' said the novelist.

The director led him around several floors. Sections of the stair-rail sprouted artfully curved copper balusters that snaked down to where their leather shoes beat out a four-step rhythm against the black marble, like two pairs of hands playing the black keys of a piano. They ascended one flight of stairs, then another, then several more. Finally, they arrived at the top floor. 'Not bad.' The attic room was small with a slanting ceiling beneath which, at the highest point, a person could easily walk up and down, and at the lowest point, were he to put a writing desk there, he would have to stoop to stand or sit. Sitting at the desk would virtually lock a person in place, ideal for someone who needed to write a lot. He gave the director his sincere thanks, 'It's ideal for work.'

The wutong tree was not as tall back then – from the attic, the novelist had to descend two floors to be able to look through the corridor windows directly at the treetop. The next floor down was the optimal spot for viewing the upper branches, and in the middle of that corridor was the break room where he installed the midrange coffee machine he'd gifted the publishing house as a token of thanks, as one might a landlord upon moving into a new residence. The new machine replaced the awful instant coffee that used to be found in there, and the novelist supplied a range of coffee beans of varying quality for a time as well. Every afternoon, after writing a little, he went downstairs to make a cup of coffee to drink with the ever-present biscuits that he ate as if he were owed them. Eventually, because of the sheer amount of coffee being consumed, the publisher started to buy their own beans, which weren't to his taste, so he stopped coming for coffee, although he continued to come for the biscuits, and for the soft sweets. On the stairs, the biscuits and sweets still close at hand, he would pause to chat with editors, both sides crystal clear on what topics were off bounds: How many characters have you written today? How much have you written already? When will you finish? The consensus among the editors: leave him to it, there's no use in hurrying things, bringing it up would only lead to embarrassment. Instead, just to be polite, they talked about the real world – weather and emerging voices in the literary scene – before returning to what they were doing.

Early on, the novelist's work hours lined up exactly with the editors' nine to five. They often spotted the back of his pensive figure, making its way along the wutong tree avenue – messenger bag over the shoulder and neatly dressed – as if he had to clock in and clock out like the rest of them. After some time, his hours shifted to 8am to 6pm, morning and evening – from then on only the most diligent editors ever saw him on the avenue. Then more time passed, and he pushed the start and end of his day further in either direction, to seven and seven – now no editors saw him arrive, or saw him leave. He gave everyone the impression that he materialised out of thin air. On the weekends, he appeared according to that same schedule. And on holidays too. Soon, one inadvertent all-nighter opened the door for countless more, and as he spent ever more time at the publishing house, he slept curled up on a sofa in the attic and even bought a simple wardrobe to keep a few clothes in. Eventually, he was there round the clock, day and night. By now the editors, particularly the younger ones who joined after he'd moved in, all shared the same unshakable misconception: the novelist was no longer a guest. He had merged with the building. He was the real head honcho, higher in status even than the director.

Still, part three of the trilogy refused to be finished.

The director verbally agreed to extend the lease twice, 'Stay a little longer, write some more. You can't rush good work.' Later, he simply kept his mouth shut and allowed the novelist to continue living there. One reason was that the room given to the novelist had been otherwise unused, so the publisher had incurred no further costs. Another was for the story. Once the right opportunity presented itself, the director planned to tip off a reporter that such-and-such novelist permanently resided in his publishing house where he wrote single-mindedly, and as his publisher, he was fully behind that decision. He was confident that the story would stew with time to become even juicier, and someday when the novel was complete and sold well, it would be people's favourite go-to anecdote, thereby fuelling word-of-mouth.

If these first two incentives demonstrated the cunning integral to any business mind, then the third reason was really quite pure and noble: the director admired the novelist. Over the years, they had become genuine close friends, and to the director's mind, the novelist was the truest embodiment of fulfilling the literary dream there was. He had met too many writers to count, big and small, yet not one possessed a tenth of the novelist's moral dedication to the art. The novelist had so devoted himself to the act of creation that he had relinquished all other aspects of life, his sole remaining material need was a poky, square room with a sofa to lay his head on, and his willpower never faltered no matter how much time passed – all qualities that the director admired. Walking the corridors of the publishing house all these years without turning over a manuscript, the novelist never showed even the slightest hint of shame and maintained a free, unencumbered demeanour. Until he ducked into the director's office that is, and the two of them shut the door; only then would his anguish spill forth from behind the mask, onto his shirt front, his knee, the floorboards, scattering everywhere like ash. He bared his heart for no one but the director, the friend who had walked with him shoulder to shoulder for so many years down this road of creation.

'This man…' The novelist sunk weakly into the chair. He had entered the office with his head high, shoulders squared – one would have been forgiven for thinking him a different species entirely to the frail-looking editors – then lowered himself down to fill the chair's back and sides. Once settled, his body started to droop and shrivel and shrink, a circle of blue cushion spreading inchmeal from under his bottom. He was talking about the dilemma of his main character, 'He needs to enter the room, the room where what sparks his whole destiny awaits him. But I don't know how to make him enter; he has been stuck in that corridor since last Friday, a whole four days.'

Sometime later, the novelist was slumped again in that same place, even more feebly, more diminutive than before, the blue cushion resembling a sea rising to half swallow the island of his rear end. He and his protagonist faced a new quandary: 'Yesterday, he made it into the room at last, then instantly I was lost again, what to do with him next? What do I do, I asked myself over and over, so many times I shifted my own anxiety onto him. In an attempt to buy some thinking time, I wrote: "Now inside the room, he asked himself, what do I do?" The moment that sentence was on the page, I hated myself thoroughly. Just because I, the writer, am simple-minded, my protagonist has turned out to be a dumb fool too. Imagine that, my sole contribution to this world, nothing but the passing on of my own imbecility into fiction. It's unforgivable.'

How the novel should unfold 'next', however, was to be the least of his worries, he could simply leave the protagonist to wait a few days in the corridor while he cogitated and, eventually, a solution would come to him. It was the already 'completed' section that was truly daunting.

As time ebbed away, so did the self that had penned the novel's very first line. Each passing day saw the novelist's views of things change, and his thinking morph beyond recognition, become that of another mind entirely. He baulked at what he had written the month before, scorned every word from the year previous, and anything written over a decade ago left him simply incredulous. He couldn't believe he had once dared to put such things down on paper. He was at war with himself, a war that saw casualties on all sides. Every moment was a tussle in which he grabbed some earlier self of his by the scruff of its neck and lambasted it about how this or that section was so badly written it needed to be torn up and restarted. But why the past self had written what it had was clear, that same self retorted; the section more than stood up to scrutiny, was well written in fact, and as the successor, it was his job to bridge the past and future, not simply to scratch a line through everything that came before. The past self made a convincing argument – by thoroughly rejecting the past, one thoroughly rejected the present too, and the future, and spending all that time rejecting things left no spare time to create. On the one hand, the selves were waging a war against each other; on the other, they simultaneously scrambled to arbitrate their own face-off as neither knew which self to declare the victor. But before a conclusive winner and loser could be announced, from a new thought emerged a new self, a new self who leapt, unhesitating, into the fray. A new self that also wished to sit in the umpire's seat – the ensuing melee was even greater than before, more chaotic and even harder to judge.

'All good writers have this problem, who doesn't doubt themselves? Doubting your work can only be a good thing,' the director gently consoled his friend, 'But I do worry about you. As I see it, writing calls for you to break out of your self-inflicted shackles, you know, transcend. Sometimes you just have to drop your scruples with your past self. You need to be truly alone, then you can take up your pen and write with abandon. That is unburdened joy.'

The novelist remained silent.

What had he been doing recently outside of 'our little trilogy'? the director asked. The novelist started to enumerate his movements in the outside world, as if recounting a previous life in outer space before touching down on earth. He was beginning to doubt whether what he was saying was true anymore.

When he'd only recently moved into the attic, the novelist still kept in touch with his friends in the arts and literary scene, but quickly 'see you later' became 'goodbye for now' became 'goodbye forever'. There was more than one occasion when he walked into a bar or coffee shop where they all were, to discover that, partly because of the change in his appearance, but mainly because it had been so long since his last public appearance, none of his old friends recognised him. He sat nearby, eavesdropped on their conversations and found the details so strange and unfamiliar, full of the names of writers he'd never heard of, of critics he didn't know, of unheard-of book marketing strategies. Before barely a few minutes he lost interest. He reduced how often he visited such places after that, and when he went, he made sure not to listen in on his old friends' conversations.

As for his home situation, he had been separate from his wife for years. 'When she wants a divorce, she'll come find me,' he told the director, 'The publishing house is easy to find.' One evening after dinner, roaming through the streets, he spied a bright-red telephone box in a secluded corner, slipped inside, fished some change out his pocket and called his wife. Hearing her voice at the other end, he said, 'It's me,' then when his wife asked how the writing was going, he wasn't sure how to answer, so said nothing. His wife changed the topic, asked how things were otherwise, he told her he had quit smoking with hardly any effort, started drinking filter coffee, and acquired a taste for jelly sweets which he ate nonstop every day. Keeping a handful of these sweets that so reminded him of his youth beside his unfinished manuscript made him feel a little better. Then his wife said his name and there was suddenly a spring in her voice. She laughed, 'It's as if you're in a different world to me, I feel like I'm on the phone with my dead husband.' Later that evening, he indeed was in another world. Lying in the attic, moonlight pouring through the small window whitening his face. He summoned his wife's voice to his mind, her face, the feeling he had had each time she read his newly written passages as he waited for her to pass judgement. He sat up to jot a few lines describing his protagonist's feelings.

What the character was doing and his most recent writer's block were both endless sources of discussion for the novelist and director. But apparently, when it came to his own life, there was nothing much he could say. He had no life to speak of. His old friends from the arts and literary scene had each moved on in their own way, leaving behind their old haunts. He never called his wife's phone again, and his wife never bothered to divorce him. He was always too busy with his writing.

Seeing how tall the wutong tree had grown, the director felt rueful. He never pressed the novelist, but time was pressing him now. At some point, the circumstances seemed to slip beyond his control. His hands were tied. He could only watch, immobilised, as the loaf of bread tipped over the table's edge. His worry had become reality. By the time the security guard had learnt to deduce the novelist's daily output from the sound of his footsteps, the novelist had reached middle age and his looks were creeping toward the geriatric. The director too was getting on, it was time for him to retire.

Behind the scenes, the director did everything in his power to help during the handover; he even sat down specially with the new director to discuss the novelist. The new director was admiring the two broad, ceiling-to-floor bookcases in the office, on which every book was one of the points of pride of the publishing house – some had been awarded national or international prizes, others had sold consistently since their release, all were carefully ordered – the way he looked at them gave the impression each was a book-shaped tombstone leaning against the wall, the two walls like sections of a cultural graveyard. Among them was the novelist's first book. As their eyes passed over it, the old director seized the opportunity to broach the subject: 'We're long accustomed to having a novelist live in the building. Myself and all the editors and other colleagues, we're all used to it. It was a little odd at first, someone sleeping and eating here, never submitting any manuscripts while we're the one invariably paying out. And it's not just the zero return either, he never tries to keep you sweet so it feels like the whole workplace is losing out – this is a place of business, we do business here! But soon enough, I started to think it was great him staying here. Between us and the novelist, it's like we've forged this old-fashioned relationship, you know like there used to be, a relationship that doesn't just hang on punctual transactions, on both parties holding up their side of the bargain. We've shed the modern insistence on seeing immediate benefits, and as a result, I've discovered certain parts of my conscience are still clean, still bright and pure as ever. I'm more broadminded, more expansive-minded than I thought. I'm surer of myself in the task at hand. When I send whatever asinine, vanity title I'm working on to the printers, when I publish some new book not worth the wood pulp it's printed on, I try to think of the novelist, and with him in mind I'm able to tell myself I'm still a dignified publisher worth my salt, who to my last day continued to promote good literature. Great literature. I'm more than qualified, and I've not a whit of regret for my career.'

'How touching! That's very touching! I hope one day to be able to look back on my own career in the same way, to speak with such magnanimity, with a clear conscience – but I've many years ahead before that. Before I can assert such things, there's considerable real work to be done. Nonetheless, your words today will long stay with me, I'm sure. I only hope that I can profess a tenth of what you have at the end of my career.' The new director spoke with forced admiration, then he asked: 'But do you actually think he writes well?'

The veteran director did not respond right away. He waited a breath to allow the asker to reflect whether or not his question might be a *faux pas*. Then he replied, yet his answer was somewhat indirect. 'It's a shame we cannot fill every role, and lucky that we don't have to. Us publishers publish. Commentary we can leave to the readers.'

The old director was driven away in a sedan car. The leaves overhead cast their shadows on the windshield, then onto his face, making the car's interior flicker between light and darkness. In the moments of dark, there were several times he had the urge to look back toward the attic easily visible over the treetops. He resisted. *There's nothing more I can do for you now. My work is done.*

The novelist had lost his champion and in no time at all, received repeated eviction notices. The new director always spoke very politely face-to-face and was never unpleasant, but he was serious about him leaving. He saw it like this, there was no other opportunity quite so convenient as this for stating his position: were he to let the novelist stay, for example, the suggestion would be that he was taking up the torch of his predecessor's thinking, his way of doing things, whereas should he ask the novelist to leave, he'd be sending an unmistakable message to the staff about his determination for reform. Both were acceptable approaches, except, considering he was relatively young, presenting a face of reform would be more advantageous to his newly ascended seat.

From then onwards, the whole publishing house, top to bottom, felt a new wind blow through it. Rules and regulations changed, the length of meetings changed, the volume people spoke at changed. But the biggest change, the one that all those swept up in the midst of this overhaul saw unfold before their eyes, was the one they saw happen to the novelist – by comparison, they were joggers watching someone else charge by at five times their speed, so fast they doubted whether they hadn't been stood in the same spot all along. The novelist's physique shifted daily, from fat to thin, young to old; even from one moment to the next during a single day, the wild metamorphoses happened too quickly to keep track. Editors would bump into him on the stairs or in the break room to find him desperately hungry for conversation, then minutes later his mouth remained sealed shut like a dead clam. There were days someone said they saw him on the second floor, only for an editor to claim they just spoke to him three floors up. And the sound of movement from the attic never stopped for a second. They tried putting themselves in his shoes: the novelist had been tormented by the new director just like everyone had; he had been pushed to both the point of making radical changes to his appearance and extreme adjustments to his writing regime. They observed another phenomenon under the new direction too, but none made the link to the novelist: biscuits and sweets in the break room were disappearing at a shocking rate, especially the sweets, as if someone were inhaling them. Virtually a moment after they were put out, they'd be gone. But because of the prevailing chaos keeping everyone occupied, no one had the presence of mind to pay proper attention, which let a lot of anomalies to pass by without a second thought.

Then one winter day, after the editors had clocked off at their usual hour and night had fallen, the novelist left the publishing house. First, he stepped through the attic door far later than usual and didn't head directly downstairs. Whatever that meant he was doing instead, the security guard heard a much richer combination of sounds than the typical pad of footsteps alone. Noises that started in the highest reaches of the attic, noises the security guard had never heard before but would later recall as like the sound of someone filling a bag with eggs and swinging them against a hard surface, cracking some and spilling their yolks and whites over the rest – the sound of that whole process combined and blended into one. Next, the security guard heard the novelist walk out his room again, linger on each floor a good while as he descended, even heading back upstairs to the attic a number of times, and all the time the security guard believing the building to be safe as ever and relaxing in his chair. When finally the novelist made his way to the ground floor, he looked especially gaunt, his expression too grave for the guard to dare strike up a conversation, at which point, it occurred to the guard, whose recent worries about his low-skilled job being put at risk had robbed him of his usual perceptiveness, that several days had passed since the novelist last left the building to eat. How he had coped was unclear. As the novelist approached, he suddenly threw the bound-up wad in his hand onto the counter where it landed with a thud, and without a word, he stalked out.

The wad was his finished manuscript.

A week later, in line with the slow pace of the publishing house, the manuscript was still to reach the first proofing stage, and the novelist had not returned to the building. An administrative staff member had been sent to check the attic, where, upon opening the door, she let out a piercing scream discordant with the long-reigning quiet expected in such workplaces, on hearing which a group of editors raced upstairs, momentarily shaking the whole building. Shortly after, someone summarised the scene inside the room, piecing together the various accounts of editors crammed into the doorway, and provided a detailed report to the new director. Several days later, news of what they'd seen finally reached the ear of the former director. Beneath the slanting ceiling, corpses strewed from the lowest end to the tallest – slumped over the desk, slouched in the chair, laid spread-eagle across the sofa, stood upright inside the simple wardrobe. And sprawled across the floor from end to end were a dozen more at least, each curled up side-by-side like ready-frozen shrimp in the supermarket. Everyone's neck was twisted, snapped. Every face was the novelist's, taken from some different point in his life between youth and middle age. Every corpse's right hand was raised, held out in front of the body, poised to write.

Racing toward an end for the novel, swarms of selves, young and old, had sprung forth from the novelist, bent on wrestling control from him. The novelist had broken the neck of every last one of them, and finally completed the manuscript.

A fortnight later, an editor opened the little cabinet door beneath the break room coffee machine to take out a paper cup for her coffee, only for another dead novelist to come tumbling out. A month later, one of the circulation department moved aside a stack of unsellable books in the corner of an unfrequented storeroom to find a heap of the novelist's corpses. Each one's right hand was raised to write, mouth open as if mid-tirade. On that final evening, with the small room already piled high with corpses, the novelist had dragged the surplus bodies to various places around the building to hide. The security guard had heard this going on but never divined the truth of what was happening.

To this day, the novelist has never shown up, and his novel is still waiting for the world's judgement. Many more corpses remain unfound in secret corners and hidden caches throughout the publishing house dappled by the waves of the wutong tree, each one another sacrifice in the name of writing.

The Story of Ah-Ming

Wang Zhanhei

Translated by Christopher MacDonald

1

THE COMMUNAL BINS ON this estate are horrendous in summer.

They reek, especially around daybreak during the season's hottest few weeks. Half-tied plastic bags of leftovers, fruit peelings and soup slops fester through the night and by morning the stench is everywhere. How to describe that smell? Imagine being on a packed bus in the morning, stewing in a fug of passenger sweat and armpit odour. Scallion-and-egg breakfast breath is in the mix, along with the occasional muffled fart expelled into the aisle. You're feeling nauseous and groggy, practically gagging on the fumes. Well, that's how it is for residents in the ground-floor flats opening directly onto the bins – it's like riding that wretched bus from the moment they get up. The smell of refuse haunts them while they're brushing their teeth, while they're having a dump and while they're eating breakfast. On it goes until someone finally sticks their head out the window and yells: 'Rubbish Man! Where the hell are you?!'

The Rubbish Man eventually shuffles over, hauling his rusty, corroded cart – though not before a dozen or so locals, heading to work on electric bikes, have voiced disgust at the stink as they sped past. A scruffy little dog, tufts of fur covering its eyes, brings up the rear. When you're waiting for the Rubbish Man, he seems to take forever dealing with the bin outside the building before yours.

Every building on the estate has a bin out front, making for about 100 bins all told, and there are dumpster sheds located every few buildings along the street. The combined web of noxious hotspots, like a network of security cameras, covers every corner of the estate.

We say the Rubbish Man *grasps* rubbish from the bins, and the character for 'grasping', 捉, happens to be visually appropriate for his task. When he turns up, he transfers rubbish from bin to cart then lays the bin down and, with a long pair of tongs, plucks out remaining scraps. One by one he retrieves stray plastic bags which have wafted away on the breeze, if they haven't blown too far. He carefully folds cardboard packaging and empties out soft drink bottles, before slipping them into his poly-fibre sack. In hot weather a rancid residue seeps from the bins, generating a tremendous stink and triggering a torrent of complaints. A sprinkler truck gets called in for part of the summer to follow-up on the Rubbish Man's round.

The same procedure is repeated step by step, bin by bin, from East to West across the entire estate. For the few dozen unfortunate families in the final buildings along the route, waiting all morning for their bins to be emptied, the stench has long since barged in and seized possession of their kitchens, living rooms and balconies. Nothing can drive it out.

One morning, towards the end of his round, what the Rubbish Man *grasped* from the bin was an old lady. It looked like she'd tumbled in and fallen asleep. When they pulled her out she smelled rank, her hair was wet with slops and there was a misshapen piece of rubber sheeting tucked down her front. As they turned her over, they realised with a gasp that it was Ah-Ming, the old lady who lived in a lock-up garage at one end of the estate.

2

When somebody changes a lot in old age we say they've *gone different*.

It generally indicates some kind of change for the worse. For example, if a man in his late seventies unexpectedly acquires a younger partner a dozen or more years after his wife died, his children say, 'He's gone different, the old goat.'

'One foot in the grave and he thinks he's stepping out on a whole new life! Disgraceful!'

Or perhaps an old chap allows himself to be so bamboozled by his good-for-nothing grandson that there's no inheritance remaining for the rest of the family. They all curse the old man's folly, damning him for the idiot he's become.

Or there's the generous-spirited woman who becomes increasingly paranoid in old age and convinces herself someone in the family wants to steal her bank deposit book. Or the retired intellectual who finds Buddha and attempts to feed his grandson incense ashes – supposedly medicinal – that he brought back from the temple. Whatever the situation, when people say an old person's *gone different* it's always something inexplicable, from a radical change in temperament to behaviour that has turned utterly bizarre.

Everyone on the estate had witnessed Ah-Ming's decline during the past few years. 'She used to be such a tidy old dear,' they'd say. 'Now look at the state of her. What a mess!'

It's generally the same kinds of people who root around in bins. There's the tramp, who is hungry and thirsty and game for whatever he can dig up. There's the migrant worker, a guy with nothing to his name, always scanning for something useful like a dumped sofa or an old pair of trainers. And then there are elderly ladies from the neighbourhood, like Ah-Ming, who collect bottles and cans along the road and trade them for a bit of cash. No-one had ever been as obsessive about the bins as Ah-Ming, though.

3

Old Ah-Ming spent more time at the bins every day than the Rubbish Man himself. She had a rummage in them when it got dark and then another go before dawn. By the time the Rubbish Man started his day, Ah-Ming had checked all the nearby bins and snaffled up anything of value. What's more, the mess she left behind was a bugger to sweep up, so the Rubbish Man loathed her. Sometimes Ah-Ming was still there when the Rubbish Man arrived and he would drive her off with his broom, hurling curses. Sometimes he was over-zealous and shoved her to the ground.

'Get away, old woman!' he bellowed, like he wanted everyone to know he'd caught her in the act. The Rubbish Man's dog had learned to detest Ah-Ming as much as he did, and charged at her whenever she came into view, barking its little head off and causing her to flee in fright.

It was Ah-Ming's neighbours who reviled her the most, though, thanks largely to her dreadful odour. In the middle of a 38° day when hardly anyone was outdoors, if you looked along the line of bins you might notice that one was at an angle. This was a sign that Ah-Ming had finished lunch and was burrowing for booty. She'd be bent over, head in the bin, and all you could see was the lower half of her body plus an old rice sack. She was busily rummaging through rubbish and stuffing things into the sack. By the time she reached the bottom of a bin, she was literally half inside it. As time went on, she herself came to exude a putrid smell. People had to pinch their noses and swerve away as they passed by. If a particularly irritable resident encountered Ah-Ming bent over the bin when he was taking out trash, he'd simply toss it over her with a glare.

Scraps of cloth, broken toys, fizzy drink cans, PVC panels – there was nothing Ah-Ming wouldn't collect. No-one knew what the old lady wanted it all for. There she was, well into her seventies, lugging a sack of crap upstairs, emptying it out, and taking it back down again. In and out throughout the day, trailing a fetid odour through the building as she shuttled between the flat upstairs and her den in the garage downstairs. The neighbours might knock on the door, ask her to clean the place up, and half-heartedly she'd toss out a few items. Unfortunately, however, there was no banishing the smell of putrescence.

It simply didn't make sense. A little old lady with a decent pension, well-known around the neighbourhood, as respectable as the next person – 'and the next thing you know she's rummaging about in filthy bins.' No-one could explain it. All anyone could say was: 'She's gone. Well and truly gone.'

4

Ah-Ming wasn't scraping by on minimum welfare support and neither was she one of those elderly folk without relatives. She was a regular person who'd had a decent job before she retired. Her husband had been a municipal warden who was killed during the holiday season one year when a street hawker went berserk and knifed him. He was in his late forties at the time. As the widow of a 'modern hero' martyred in the line of duty, Ah-Ming received a stipend which helped to put her son, Ah-Hsin, through vocational college.

Ah-Hsin had a lucky break when he graduated. He slotted into his father's old post and began earning his crust as a municipal warden, albeit with little enthusiasm. He used to say: 'What's the point of all this 'cracking down' on traders? You're out there rain or shine and can't even pocket what you confiscate! Me, I'm gonna grease some palms, pull a few strings. Before you know it, I'll be in a cushy office job!' It never happened, though.

Within a few years, Ah-Hsin found himself a wife. They couldn't afford their own place so they squeezed in with his mother in the 60-square-metre, two-room flat; one room for her and one for them. The young couple went out to work and Ah-Ming cooked at home. Everything was dandy. Then her son had a son and the flat became too small for them all. Ah-Ming offered to move into the garage downstairs. They cleaned it up, fitted a window and put in a bed. The old lady seemed comfortable enough down there. By day she took care of the cooking and looked after the child, in the flat upstairs. After dinner, once she'd washed the dishes and put the child down, she'd go back downstairs. All of them were looking forward to the day their number came up for affordable housing, so that Ah-Hsin and his wife could move out.

The other old ladies were indignant on Ah-Ming's behalf. 'Squatting in the garage instead of sleeping in your own family's flat,' they said. 'You shouldn't have to put up with that!' Ah-Ming waved away their concerns. 'Never mind. When our Ah-Hsin gets his flat I'll have the whole place to myself.' She went on saying this for years but nothing changed, so she remained in the poky little garage on the ground floor.

Luckily Ah-Ming was resourceful and had no problem getting the little space neatly sorted. The neighbours marvelled when they dropped by for a look. The camp bed, with its blanket and mosquito net, made a pretty little picture. There was a small television set under a dust cover, and photographs and a calendar on the wall. There was a little dining table with two chairs and just enough space so as not to feel cramped. Some of the other old girls used to come and sit in the space in front of the garage, gabbling merrily about everything and everyone. It was like a scene from the old days.

'It's good being on the ground floor,' Ah-Ming told people. 'Saves you having to schlep upstairs. Feels like being back in one of the old single-storey houses.'

Women from the wool factory really get into their needlework after they retire. They meet up to admire each other's pieces of fabric and compare techniques, chatting about different methods for seaming and tying off thread. Ah-Ming had an old-fashioned sewing machine which she cherished more than anything. It was in fine condition despite its antique appearance, and she kept it polished and shiny under a snug-fitting cotton cover. Being a deft seamstress, Ah-Ming could make do with the least costly materials. She selected offcuts at the shop, washed and dried them, then made them into whatever worked best. The family's pillow covers, her son's pyjamas, her grandson's cloth nappies and her own clothes – all were treadle-sewn on Ah-Ming's machine. Leftover scraps could always be bundled into mop heads. Hats and gloves for winter were knitted from cheap balls of wool. The family saved plenty in clothing costs.

The child grew quickly, and with each change of season Ah-Ming put in extra hours at the sewing machine. Within a few days, fresh little socks and shorts would be hanging on the balcony, a size larger than the ones before.

5

There was still no sign of an office job for Ah-Hsin after five or six years, so he eventually quit as a warden and went into business with a partner. Trade was slow, a new flat hadn't come through yet and the child was due to start nursery. Money was getting tighter. It must have been around then that Ah-Ming had the idea of collecting scrap.

There was a dumpster shed diagonally across from Ah-Ming's garage, and drinkers tended to lob empties at it during the night, not bothering where they landed. It meant the ground was strewn with bottles and cans when Ah-Ming raised her door each morning. She gathered the intact items into an old rice sack, and it wasn't long before the sack was full. At the end of the month, she exchanged the contents for cash at the Minfang Grocery. She recouped a few more pennies on what remained from a local scrap collector, who came by on his three-wheeled cart and paid by weight.

Evidently, Ah-Ming had found a way to help out, and her daughter-in-law thought so too – 'Every little bit counts'. Ah-Ming took to walking around the estate when she had time during the day, checking corners near the bin sheds for discarded soft drink bottles. At the same time, she'd help herself to promotional leaflets from people's letterboxes, along with their old newspapers. Other people who collected scrap in the area got to know Ah-Ming well and told her about the estates with the worst refuse collection and the roads with the best pickings. Ah-Ming started roaming further afield and collecting even more scrap. Leaflets were often in Ah-Ming's hands only moments after being stuffed into a letterbox, and sometimes she made off with people's newly delivered newspapers and utility bills in the process. If anyone saw her they'd cry: 'Oi, old woman! What d'you think you're doing?'

The tellings-off didn't faze her. It was all money at the end of the day. Bundled waste paper and loaded sacks – Ah-Ming's precious property – were neatly stacked in front of the garage. Every day neighbours would spot her at various points around the estate, and in the park and at the wholesale market. When she went for groceries at the local market she always took a spare sack along and had a scout around. Plenty of people went out of their way to be kind to her. 'Hey Ah-Ming, don't wear yourself out, now. You've got to look after yourself. Let your son and daughter-in-law worry about bringing in the banknotes!'

Ah-Ming laughed it off. 'It's nothing – running around like this is good for me. Great exercise!'

Gradually, Ah-Ming came to be sighted in more and more places. Neighbours would spot her out on the streets in the scorching summer heat and on frigid winter days. It wasn't a nice thing to see, but then what could you do? 'Every family has its cross to bear, after all. The whole clan is beggared if people can't take a bit of hardship.'

6

Old Ah-Ming was roaming further from home and coming back even later, and while Ah-Hsin didn't object he wasn't exactly happy with the situation. For one thing, it was embarrassing. Everyone could see her traipsing about, a mother sent out by her son to collect scrap to support the family. People would be laughing about it. And to add to that, she was falling behind on the shopping and cooking. When the child came home he'd wail that he was hungry, and then Ah-Hsin would get mad.

'No-one's making you go around collecting scrap! Stop it now! It makes us look terrible. Stay home and look after the child. Food on the table three times a day, that's what you need to worry about. Got it?'

Ah-Hsin always barked out orders. It wasn't worth talking back.

The old lady agreed to stop, but furtively carried on. She took a shopping bag to market but came back with an extra sack of pickings. When people hailed her on the street it used to be: 'Ah-Ming, you're back from the market!' Now it was more like: 'Ah-Ming, you've got some new stock in!' She would let out an uncomfortable laugh, then scuttle off to stash her haul as quickly as possible. She was like a thief hiding stolen goods. Some of what she brought back was packed away outside the back window and some at the bottom of the stairwell. Kids found her collection of soft drink bottles under a stone bench and started kicking them around. Ah-Ming went after them to get the bottles back. 'Little wretches! Who said you could touch those?'

Slowly it dawned on people that Ah-Ming was collecting increasingly random items. 'She brings it all back with her, sellable or not.' That's how the scrap collector with the three-wheeler put it. He was kicking himself for getting involved with her in the first place. Now he couldn't pass the garage without being dragged over. 'Come and have a look, come and have a look.'

'I've told the old lady time and again you can't sell this kind of material,' he said. 'It just won't sell. But she keeps on collecting it.' As the frown on his face indicated, Ah-Ming had become a big nuisance for him and his operation, as well as for everyone else.

People shook their heads. They muttered about what was up with Ah-Ming but never let anything slip in front of her son. He had such a vile temper.

Eventually an affordable flat came through for Ah-Hsin and his wife. They scraped together the down-payment and got busy fitting out the new place, leaving their son's daily routine in Ah-Ming's hands. Within a few days someone worked up the courage to tell Ah-Hsin that they'd seen Ah-Ming and the boy scavenging for waste on a building site. 'Ceramic tiles, fluorescent tubes, that sort of thing.' Ah-Hsin hurtled home, furious. He went straight to the garage where he saw the mass of junk. Ah-Ming put on a smile and was about to show him what everything was for when he launched into an angry tirade.

'The new flat's mine and fitting it up is my business. You're not paying for it and you're not to get involved. Grubbing around for other people's dregs like this when you're old enough to be dead. What a disgrace!

'Be senile all you want, but dragging the child into it — what the hell were you thinking?!'

It was around dinner time and Ah-Hsin had a booming voice, so all the neighbours heard. He went upstairs, slammed the door, and never let Ah-Ming take the child out on her own again.

7

Who knows if Ah-Hsin's rant deterred the old lady or spurred her on? Either way, it was a humiliation. People tutted and talked about her as she crossed the estate. Like Ah-Hsin, they assumed she must have lost the plot. 'Picked up so much junk she's gone soft in the head.'

When people noticed random objects stuffed into bushes, or crammed into corners and under benches they said, 'Look, it's Ah-Ming's stockpile!'

And whenever a freshly delivered newspaper went astray everyone said the same thing: 'Ah-Ming's probably got it!'

But Ah-Ming continued busying about, unconcerned. Cash-deposit bottles and cans were no longer enough for her. She rummaged meticulously through every bin, one after another, in search of whatever was available. Big or small, fish tank or mop head, it was all fair game and it all went back home with her. From breakfast to dinner she was out all day, roaming with her sack. Sometimes she strayed onto a national highway or took the wrong bus and didn't get back until the middle of the night.

In the morning, people would notice a new heap of junk in front of the garage. 'No, no… not for sale,' she'd say. She'd set out a basin and flask and wash each item, one by one, refilling a bucket at the river when she ran out of water. Then she'd spread them all out, like exhibits, to dry on the bare ground.

'This is a perfectly good stool. The kids can use it once it's been cleaned up. This piece of cloth, it's going to make a beautiful curtain.' She smiled at the passers-by, explaining where each piece came from and what it was good for.

No-one wanted to risk getting drawn into conversation with Ah-Ming, or trying to reason with her, so they just hurried past with a noncommittal word or two. After a while, it was easier to simply pretend they hadn't seen her. The scrap collector on the three-wheeler now gave her garage a wide berth, and the other old girls, her former colleagues, stopped calling by when they were getting together for a sewing session. The space in front of Ah-Ming's garage was now mostly deserted. Just her sitting alone on the ground, sorting her items, then washing them, then sorting again.

Ah-Hsin and his wife had long-since stopped Ah-Ming shopping and cooking for them, and didn't even allow her up to the flat. Ah-Hsin's wife thought she was dirty and worried about the child catching germs. After dinner, Ah-Hsin would take a pan of leftovers downstairs and transfer the contents into the old lady's bowl, for her to eat alone in the garage. It was the same routine, every day. If she wasn't there, Ah-Hsin placed the bowl of food on the ground outside the garage, where the dogs soon got it.

One day, probably because she'd sold off some stock or scavenged something precious, Ah-Ming was looking particularly pleased. She went to market with her little cloth bag and came back with half a sauce-braised duck. 'Ooh, special treat today, Ah-Ming!' said people at the entrance to the estate. Ah-Ming smiled back: 'My grandson loves this!'

Since she couldn't go upstairs, Ah-Ming kept watch

outside the garage until the boy came home from school. She waved him over: 'Here, my sweet! Gran's bought us something nice!' The two of them tucked in, each taking a bite in turn. At just that moment, however, Ah-Ming's daughter-in-law arrived back from work. She snatched the duck leg from the child's hand, flung it into the weeds, and slapped him across the face.

'So you like that filth do you? Dirty swine! Upstairs, now!' The hapless child was dragged away in tears, leaving Ah-Ming sitting where she was. Not a word of reproach had been directed at her by the boy's mother. Not a single word.

Just like the neighbours, Ah-Ming's daughter-in-law looked right through her.

8

Ah-Hsin and his wife moved out with their child as soon as the new place was ready. They took the furniture and left Ah-Ming with an empty flat. Minus their contents, the two rooms seemed big and spacious. Ah-Ming stayed on in her compact little garage on the ground floor, however. She never went upstairs to sleep.

Before long, the flat was jammed with junk. While Ah-Ming lived downstairs, the place upstairs became her storeroom. Every item she collected, no matter what, was stashed away there. There was no more sorting and cleaning – she didn't have time for that. She bustled out as soon as she woke in the morning and didn't get back until dark. Where she went, what she ate, no-one knew.

Someone quipped, 'Ah-Ming even gets dinner from the bins now!' When people ran into her on the street they called out, 'Hey, Ah-Ming, better get some new stock in!' Others said 'Yo, Ah-Ming, off to work then!'

The old lady, grimy from head to toe, quietly responded:

'Things to go and see. I've got some things to go and see.' Then headed off to who knows where.

By now, most of the neighbours simply ignored Ah-Ming, having long since passed the stage of feeling sorry for her. To them, she was like a rag-picker or tramp. A batty old lady, someone with no family to speak of who'd clearly lost her marbles. She didn't even come up to the level of the Rubbish Man because she didn't collect refuse. She had no idea what she was collecting.

On one occasion, she was taken to hospital clutching her stomach in agony, looking deathly pale. Because no relatives came to claim her, she was on Community News the following day. It turned out she'd given herself food poisoning by drinking from a bottle she'd picked up at the train station. When the reporter asked her about it, she mumbled something about a sweet little boy who'd smiled at her, and how she'd wanted to give him a drink. She'd sipped from the bottle first to check it was all right, and instantly felt queasy.

Ah-Ming had a gastric tube inserted and was put on a drip, but the drink bottle had been thrown away so the doctors couldn't determine what she'd drunk. Pesticide? Liquid detergent? They just had to deal with it as best they could. In the news clip, Ah-Ming groaned 'It hurts… my throat's burning.' But there were no tears and she wasn't kicking up a fuss.

Ah-Hsin came and signed the old lady out of hospital. He took her back to the estate and, without further ado, left her there. The garage door was wide open and passers-by could see her lying on the camp bed. Everyone knew what had happened but no-one went in to ask how she was. The dogs strayed in at one point and she flailed her arms to shoo them out. Fortunately, she didn't seem to be in such a bad way, aside from her sickly pallor. When it was dark, she got up and sat quietly on the bed. She lit a dim lamp, went upstairs to get something from the flat, then hurried back down.

Within a few days, Ah-Ming had her strength back and was out and about with her sack. After that, there were often nights when no light at all glimmered from the garage.

'Ah-Ming must have died out there,' people said. But a few days later she'd be back on the estate.

9

On this particular night, Ah-Ming had rummaged about in the bins for too long at the end of a boiling hot day and had finally succumbed. Maybe because it was airless in those bins, or just too smelly. But this time she didn't end up in hospital. 'Motherfucker!' exclaimed the Rubbish Man as he dragged her out. People heading to work stopped for a look, pinching their noses as they approached, then hastily backing off from the stench. The Rubbish Man prodded Ah-Ming with his foot and got his dog to have a sniff. She lay motionless.

Someone said, 'Quick! Call 1-2-0! Get an ambulance!'

'What's the point?' someone else said. 'Call Ah-Hsin. Tell him to come and get the body!'

A little crowd formed, standing well back from the inert figure under its cloud of flies. A rancid fluid spread across the ground towards them.

The Rubbish Man went to the river, returned with a bucket of water and emptied it over Ah-Ming.

After a couple of moments, she came to.

She wasn't dead, so the Rubbish Man moved on to the next building and the gawkers quickly dispersed. They had to get away from that smell. Ah-Ming had rummaged through so many bins she was like a walking refuse tip.

'Face to face with the living dead first thing in the morning! Talk about bad omens!' Muttering grimly, everyone steered around the bin and skirted the patch of ground where

Ah-Ming had lain. But there wasn't a single bin on the estate that Ah-Ming hadn't foraged at some point, and there was no way off the estate without passing her garage. There was no getting around Ah-Ming. Wherever some item had been disposed of by some person, Ah-Ming had been there. Whatever it was, Ah-Ming wanted it.

It was just no-one wanted Ah-Ming. Only the bins wanted her now. Recyclable rubbish and non-recyclable rubbish, it was all the same to her. The bins gave Ah-Ming food and they gave her shelter. They gave her everything she desired. And this past night, in the big green bin, she'd slept so blissfully well.'

Ah-Ming stood up, patted herself down and returned to her garage. Beaming with pleasure she pulled out the shiny sewing machine. 'Now then, let's have a look. What a first-rate material. Just the thing for disposable nappies.'

Ah-Ming tugged the mildewed sheet of rubber from her front and began lightly working the treadle.

The Lost

Fu Yuehui

Translated by Carson Ramsdell

LOOKING BACK ON IT, Gu Lingzhou realised that prior to the whole thing starting, there had been several warning signs. He'd just turned a blind eye to them. What he'd taken for a benevolent smile, was in fact fate baring vicious fangs.

To begin with, there was something not quite right about the alarm on his phone that morning. It seemed so quiet, and only when this thought crossed his mind did its chiming grow to a deafening crescendo.

As soon as he arrived at the office his boss made a beeline for him, saying an author had just called complaining about his negative attitude when discussing a book cover the day before. He conjured up an image of the author in his head and cursed her. Some nerve! Going over his head like that.

Answering his boss, Gu Lingzhou headed for the water cooler to grab a cup of Tie Guan Yin oolong. He bowed his head and watched the purling steam hovering above his cup, his boss's words churning somewhere in its midst, their sting dissolving slightly. Suddenly, he looked up at his boss and smiled.

'I understand. It won't happen again.'

His boss obviously hadn't finished speaking, but interrupted and losing his thread, he begrudgingly replied with some hackneyed retort about Gu Lingzhou being too young and inexperienced.

That's when Gu Lingzhou's phone rang.

He looked at the number. A landline, but he didn't recognise it. Plugging his earphones in, he made a swift exit. Out on the office balcony, he allowed his gaze to come to rest on the top of the camphor tree in the courtyard before answering.

It was a woman's voice. Though he'd no idea whose.

'Could you do me a favour?' she asked. Her voice had a rasp like wind whispering across sand. Judging by the sound of it, she wasn't young. He guessed maybe thirty-five, thirty-six. The kind of woman who was getting on in years. Of no interest to him. He met a lot of people through his job, and there was no way he was going to save all their numbers in his phone. Often calls were simply strings of digits. But as he didn't like asking names right off the bat, he asked, 'What do you need?'

The woman on the other end hesitated, and in a hushed tone replied, 'Can you come get me? I'm lost.'

Gu Lingzhou held his phone, stupefied. Shanghai was big. Little kids and the elderly probably got lost on the daily, but a thirty-something-year-old… How could a woman her age possibly get lost?

Regardless, he decided to ask where she was.

'I don't know. If I knew that I wouldn't have to bug you now, would I?'

Perplexed he said, 'Well, can you at least give me a district? Some kind of recognisable architecture near you?'

A pause. She was probably taking in her surroundings.

'Jinshan,[1] I guess… There's really not much around here at all. Just some houses.'

'… How about a street sign then?'

The woman was obviously distressed.

'I don't know! I can't see any street signs. I asked some people but their answers were all over the place. I can't find my phone or wallet, and I don't even have enough for a bus fare on me, just enough to make this call. So are you gonna come get me or not?! You better get over here. I'm waiting right here till you do.'

The woman's voice gradually broke into a sob.

Chewed out like that for nothing. Gu Lingzhou was miffed.

'How am I supposed to find you if you can't give me anything to go on?!'

A whimper-studded pause came through from the other end before the woman gradually calmed down.

Level-headed once more, she said, 'I'm calling from a corner shop. There's a camphor tree out front that you can see from real far off. A big camphor tree!'

He couldn't help feeling that odd mixture of frustration and amusement. There was no telling how many camphor trees there were in Shanghai!

Without warning, a camphor tree began to manifest itself before his eyes, even more robust, sumptuous and weatherworn than the one standing before him in the courtyard.

He let out a callous, exasperated snicker.

'Then at the very least, you gotta give me your name?'

The other end went silent. You could literally hear her come to a grinding halt.

Gu Lingzhou held his phone, ears pricked, ready for her response. 'Pffff… I guess I must have dialled the wrong number then,' came the woman's reply.

He could hear the disappointment in her voice. There was no 'guessing' about it; she most certainly had the wrong number. He let out a sigh. To think he'd drivelled on and on with a stranger for this long.

'So… are you coming then?' asked the woman feebly.

First, she says she has the wrong number, now she asks him to go pick her up again! Is she out of her mind?

'Right away!' he bellowed, before immediately hanging up and sliding his phone shut.

'Oof…'

He liked the feel of this type of phone. There was a certain decisiveness to opening and closing it. He'd bought it less than a month ago after he'd taken a liking to precisely this feature.

Gu Lingzhou took another look at the tree in the courtyard, and again a vision of a plush, gnarly camphor tree unwittingly burgeoned forth, blooming verdant behind his eyes. It was only with a wrinkle of his brow and a shake of his head that he managed to banish the apparition.

He went back, plopped down in front of his computer and, without really thinking about it, looked up the area code the woman had called from. It was, in fact, from Jinshan. Before long though, he forgot about the whole ordeal.

Sipping his tea, he returned to work with robotic precision. His tasks for the day consisted mainly of checking the covers of two books. This wasn't particularly difficult and should've been quick work for him, but he was dragging his feet. No matter how he adjusted the colours, something always seemed off. Even when he'd finally finished, restlessness, despondence and boredom set in. Something just seemed off.

Gu Lingzhou sifted through the towering stacks of books and newspapers on his desk and discovered an unopened parcel from the weekly paper. Upon tearing it open, he discovered it featured two of the four-frame comic strips he'd drawn. He struggled to remember exactly when he'd submitted them. Reading them again, he was surprised and a little embarrassed to find himself laughing at his own stale jokes. Before long, though, what began with him reading his own comic strips segued somehow into reading the whole paper.

Right next to his strip, an unremarkable article happened to catch his eye: it was about tourists losing things on the Shanghai subway – mostly phones and cameras. The reporter who penned the piece came up with a clever little nickname for tourists of this ilk: 'muddleheads'. Although Gu Lingzhou wasn't what you might call meticulous, he certainly didn't feel he was a muddlehead. He imagined those phone-bereft out-of-towners, city-virgins plunged wide-eyed into this colossal, unfamiliar city only to lose their phones immediately. What would come of that? Separated from their families with no way to get in touch with them. He'd never actually seen anyone lost out there on the streets. That was the real miracle. With so many people losing their phones, none of them seemed to get lost themselves.

Mind racing, he snatched his phone from his desk to take a look. Sometimes, when riding the subway, he'd wonder what would happen if he lost *his* phone. The second this thought sprouted in his head he gripped the phone tightly as a faint sense of anxiety washed over him. If that really were to happen – if he really did lose his phone – how many people would actually go to the ends of the earth in search of him?

Gu Lingzhou fiddled with his phone. This sort of thing happened to other people, not to him, he told himself. But his phone didn't leave his hand for a moment all day, lest some disaster befalls him.

After lunch, he sprawled out in his office chair and, still clutching his phone, thought again about the woman who'd called him three hours earlier. Was she still waiting for him? He guessed not. If she was still waiting, she'd probably have called him again by now. Lots of people who dialled the wrong number did that – call again and again, that is – only letting up when they'd called one too many times and he'd lost his temper. By this logic, it would only be natural that the woman would keep calling... But she didn't. What was she doing under that camphor tree right now? No sooner had the thought crossed his mind than the wild vision of that tree's leaves and branches mosaiced their way through his head. There was no stopping them this time. He imagined the scene. Some woman lost in Shanghai, standing under a camphor tree outside a corner shop, gazing up into the branches.

It was some time before the ping of a text message tore Gu Lingzhou from his reverie. He couldn't believe it. He'd actually sprawled across his desk and passed out for a minute. The text was from his girlfriend. She said she was talking with her parents, and wanted to know if he missed her. She'd been back home for a week and had been sending messages asking, 'Do you miss me? Do you miss me? Do you miss me?' from the moment she boarded the train. His responses had a certain variability compared with the consistency of her inquiries. A 'Yeah' here, a 'Miss you' there. Sometimes simply an ambiguous 'Lol'. But now he was getting tired of it. They were like an old married couple. What the hell was there to 'miss' anyway? In fact, when she'd left, he felt relieved. He knew it wasn't quite right, but he actually felt liberated. He wanted to have a little fun. So, he snuck a few texts out to some female friends whom he'd previously had ambiguous relationships with. What he hadn't considered was that each of their responses would come in more formal than the last. Demoralised, he realised just why it was that he'd prattled on with that woman for so long.

After a while, he finally decided to shoot his girlfriend a two-word response. 'Of course!' – something he never said. 'That's more like it!' she quickly replied.

They had started living together right after he finished his undergrad degree at 23 – about four years ago – something he now greatly regretted. After living together for so long, he no longer had the heart for marriage. Of course, had they got married straight away, he would never have had it in him to get a divorce. This was precisely what was on his mind when he began penning comic strips about relationships for the paper. His publisher had informed him that many of his readers noted a stylistic similarity with Zhu Deyong's work.[2] As far as he was concerned, he was just drawing what felt true to life. He always used a pen name of course. He couldn't let his boss discover his irreverence toward his actual job. Even worse would be if his girlfriend found out. His girlfriend didn't understand, or frankly didn't want to understand, artistic imagination. She'd sniff out all sorts of trivialities from his cartoons and deduce that he'd had a string of affairs.

Head still churning, Gu Lingzhou's phone chimed. For a split second, he assumed it was the woman again, but on answering it discovered it was his friend Lao Han. He couldn't help but feel a little disappointed. It seemed he *was* waiting for the woman to call again after all.

'You didn't forget about dinner tonight, did you?' asked Lao Han.

'No...' he replied, trying hard to remember what time they'd decided on.

'Well, me and the other two guys have something to take care of. We'll have to push it back half an hour or so. Sorry.'

It was only then that he remembered that he'd made plans with two other friends as well as Lao Han that night. He followed up with a, 'No problem,' and Lao Han hung up.

Gu Lingzhou and his friends would usually plan dinners for 5:30. Normally at a big place called the Fuyuan Inn.

He checked the time. If Lao Han and the other guys hadn't been running late, he wouldn't have made it even if he left now. Time had flown by. It was nearly 5 o'clock, and it'd take two hours to make his way over to the restaurant. He quietly put his things in order, grabbed his phone and headset and hurried downstairs out of the office. He'd have to get a cab to the subway station.

Not long after, he'd replay this stretch of time again and again, and be unable to find even the slightest split in the procedural seams. In fact, on the contrary, he'd clearly recall wondering if the woman was still standing under the camphor tree as he picked up his phone to leave the office, and decided to relay the whole episode to his friends over dinner.

Next, at the front of his office building, Gu Lingzhou hailed a cab. He would later recall with unmistakable certainty that it was a blue cab. Not green, not red. Blue. When the cab pulled over to stop, he realised there was someone sitting inside. At first the guy inside didn't budge. He was waiting for the receipt. Thinking back on it, Gu Lingzhou would question whether or not he seemed impatient. The moment the passenger received his slip and opened the door to step out, Gu Lingzhou pushed his way into the cab, brushing against the alighting passenger as he did so. Had the other guy looked at him? Probably not. Gu Lingzhou sat down next to the driver, hugged his backpack against his chest and told him to head to the nearest Line 1 station.

Yes. This was *exactly* how everything played out.

It was super congested. He wanted to slip a magazine he carried with him out of his backpack to peruse but was distracted by some unforgettable scenery sliding past his window. He'd been down this road many times before but had never noticed just how distinctive the view was. So, he left the magazine in his backpack and watched the spectacle unspool before him, until he gradually realised there was, in fact, nothing special about it at all. He decided to pull the magazine out of his bag and thumb through it. When he'd got about halfway through – yes, that was it – he suddenly realised his phone was missing.

Everything was going to be alright. He'd run through this scenario countless times before in his head. He felt in his pockets – nothing. He rummaged through every inch of his bag – nothing. Went back through his pockets – still nothing. He wasn't worried though, not yet.

'Could you turn around, please?' he asked the driver. 'I left my phone at the office.'

Without hesitation, the driver pulled a U-turn and headed back toward Gu Lingzhou's place of work. As soon as they were headed the other way, the road seemed to open up. He remembered asking the driver why there was so little traffic headed this way.

'You're lucky it was so congested a minute ago. Otherwise, there's no telling where we'd've been by this point,' said the driver, disregarding his question.

Gu Lingzhou agreed and asked the driver to wait for him, adding that his office was just right next to the road.

'Sure,' the driver conceded.

Gu Lingzhou dashed out of the taxi straight for his office upstairs. He remembered speculating as to why the driver trusted him to just go without paying. Wasn't he afraid he just wanted a free ride and came up with some excuse? No, he thought. Couldn't be. Who would get a ride just to circle back around to where they came from? His brain was in overdrive. He pushed open the door to the office. His boss hadn't left yet.

'What're you doing back?' his boss asked.

Gu Lingzhou said he'd forgotten his phone, and began turning over the books on his desk, searching. The phone was nowhere to be found. A slight panic started to set in. He went back through his day, hastily checking everywhere he'd been inside the office. Still nothing.

'I've lost my phone,' he finally admitted.

'How'd you lose it?' his boss inquired, dropping what he was doing.

Gu Lingzhou recounted the whole story, start to finish. It was all so straightforward. There wasn't much to say.

'Well, if it's not in the office, then its probably in the taxi,' his boss advised. Gu Lingzhou asked him to call the phone. His boss agreed. He recited the number as his boss dialled simultaneously. After his boss misheard him a couple times, Gu Lingzhou anxiously wrenched the phone out of his hands and dialled himself.

At long last he got through... only for the sound of a busy signal to fill his ears. His boss hung up. Dialled again. Just like that, the phone had been turned off.

'Well, looks like someone took it,' surmised his boss.

Gu Lingzhou tore off for the taxi parked below. Perhaps he'd left it there. He ran downstairs. Sure enough, the taxi stood right where he left it, only it had turned around. He dove into the car informing the driver that his phone wasn't up in the office and asked him to call his phone.

'Fine, fine...' muttered the driver, pulling out his phone.

The driver, however, kept misdialling. Annoyed, Gu Linzhou said he'd do it himself, before snatching the driver's phone and dialling.

'We're sorry, you have reached a number that has been disconnected.'

Thinking back on it, he felt he'd made plenty of errors in his rushing about. Everything he'd done was so impulsive and careless. How could he have only thought to check inside the taxi this late? Naturally, it wasn't in there either. With stark lucidity, he questioned whether he *had* really lost his phone? He furrowed his brow. He'd better get out of the car and go look for his phone in the office. He was slightly more mindful exiting the taxi, however, taking down the driver's employee I.D. number pasted above the glovebox: 128537. Then, with a swipe of his transit card, he paid his fare and hastily began to make his way back to the office, not even bothering to take the receipt.

'Lookin' pretty busy today, Ol' Gu,' joked the attendant in the security hut at the entrance to the office parking lot.

The guard's words went unheard as Gu Lingzhou made his way straight for his office to perform another search. His phone had to reappear at some point. But it didn't. It was only at this point that the severity of the situation began to set in. In all his seven years using a mobile, this was the first time he'd ever lost one.

Now, his boss was worried too. He went through the sequences of events over and over, concluding it must have slipped out of Gu Lingzhou's pocket when he boarded the taxi, and asked whether or not he'd got a receipt. Upon learning he hadn't, his boss asked him what the hell he'd been thinking. At the very least, he'd taken down the driver's employee I.D., he told his boss.

'We can work with that. Which company was it? Dazhong? Call 114 and check Dazhong.'

Gu Lingzhou called 114. The car wasn't Dazhong's.

'How about Ba-shi?'

Gu Lingzhou dialled a second time. It wasn't Ba-shi either. The person from Ba-shi was blunt. 'There's absolutely no way that's our car. No reason to even check. Ba-shi Taxi Co. doesn't have any blue vehicles. All of our vehicles are green, and they wouldn't be picking up fares downtown. There are over 100 cab companies in Shanghai, it may be another company, but it's definitely not ours.'

Hearing this left Gu Lingzhou in a stupor. Could there really be that many cab companies? He called 114 again to inquire about a cab driver complaint line, wrote it down and dialled. The representative listened to his story, asked for the employee I.D. and told Gu Lingzhou they'd call back in a moment. After a few minutes, the phone rang saying the I.D. belonged to a Ba-shi driver.

Gu Lingzhou hung up and dialled Ba-shi once again. The Ba-shi employee informed him with 100 per cent confidence that it was simply not possible that the I.D. number was theirs. Gu Lingzhou countered that he'd received this information from the complaint hotline.

'Then maybe it was an illegal cab,' parried the representative. 'I suggest you call the Traffic Management Bureau.'

Again, Gu Lingzhou called 114, who informed him that there wasn't any bureau by that name on record, but they could provide him with an alternative complaint line. The number they gave him, however, was the same one that had just told him the employee I.D. was Ba-shi's. He called them again anyway but was met with the same response. By this point he was pissed off.

'Then call the police.'

Furious, he dialled 110, where the dispatcher instructed him to go to the nearest police station. So, he checked in again with 114 to get the number for the nearest police station, which he dialled, but was told that even if his phone was lost in the cab, as long as the driver didn't steal it, it only counted as a civil case, not a criminal one and as such a police report could not be filed. He should call the department that handles illegal cab crimes.

'And what agency is that?' Gu Lingzhou pushed.

The officer who'd picked up the phone asked the person next to him and said, 'The Traffic Management Bureau?'

Gu Lingzhou slumped crestfallen into his swivel chair. There was no chance of finding his phone at this point, he thought. Just that morning, he'd vividly recounted looking through his contacts. 534. He currently had 534 numbers saved in his phone. 534 little threads woven into the fabric of his life, plucked right out in an instant. He was hit with a paradoxical sense of calm. Could the person he'd bumped shoulders with on his way into the cab have taken it? He quickly rejected the notion. Impossible. That guy had barely brushed him on his way out of the car. If it had been him, it would've been like a scene from a movie. The only other person he'd come into contact with was the cab driver. He struggled to remember what the driver had looked like. He remembered he'd been 50-something, amiable and with a thin face. When he'd said he had to go back for his phone, the driver agreed without a fuss. On the way back to the office, the driver had even asked him what the deal with Bluetooth was as well. Without a doubt, the driver seemed fine, not at all like the kind of person who'd steal his phone.

But mulling it over, Gu Lingzhou began to think his boss had the right idea. Maybe the taxi driver *had* taken it. When he'd gone back inside the office the first time, the driver might have found it, and after they'd called and gotten through the first time, shut it off. As he pondered this notion, the driver's once genial countenance mutated into something more nefarious. Why was it, then, that he couldn't find the driver either? After so many phone calls, not a trace of the driver had been found. In a modern city like Shanghai, amidst the immense convenience of an information age, should it really be this difficult to find somebody?

In the middle of giving him his latest piece of advice, Gu Lingzhou's boss asked him whether or not he'd taken down the wrong I.D. number. He heard it but didn't process it. He decided to head out. His phone was lost and there was nothing he could do about it. He called China Mobile, gave his name and I.D. number and suspended his service. Then he slung his backpack over his shoulder and walked disconsolately down the spiral staircase.

The elderly attendant in the security station gave a wrinkly smile.

'What's got you all tied up today, Ol' Gu?'

'I lost my phone.'

'Really can't find it, eh?'

'Yep, really can't find it…' and for some reason even he didn't understand, he let out a little laugh.

As he stood once again at the door to the office building and hailed a cab, for a second he imagined himself hopping in some taxi and chasing after his phone, straight out of some Hollywood car chase. He chuckled at his little fantasy. Back in yet another cab, Gu Lingzhou sensed keenly life's sporadic and unanticipated fluctuations. This blubbery-faced driver kept digging at his teeth with a toothpick. He didn't give off the best impression, but Gu Lingzhou was still unable to restrain himself from relaying the whole losing-his-phone-in-another-taxi story. He'd made up his mind: his phone had gone missing in that taxi. Mid-pick, the corpulent cabby explained that he usually returned anything he found to his passengers. Adding, 'How much is a phone worth anyway? It's the information that you store on it that really matters.' The driver advised him to give such and such a place a ring.

'Yeah, but what are the chances that'll do any good, right?' Gu Lingzhou asked.

'You never know. Whether or not you can see it now, most people in this world are alright.'

Gu Lingzhou nodded, thinking to himself, 'Yeah, but don't you just *usually* give back the stuff you find? What about the times that aren't so *usual*?'

As soon as he stepped inside Fuyuan Inn, Lao Han and the others boisterously set about trying to get him to drink, make up for lost time.

'Where the hell were you? Let's have it!' Lao Han joked.

'Where else would I have been? Something came up.'

For a second, Gu Lingzhou wanted to tell them a woman called him after she'd lost her phone and wallet. He'd gone to get her and got held up. He wasn't sure why he had the urge to lie like that. But just as he was about to spit it out, Gu Lingzhou choked it back and told them a co-worker had lost her phone just as he was about to leave, and he had to help her look for it.

'Did you find it then?' Lao Han asked, uninterested, as he refilled Gu Lingzhou's glass of beer, from which merely a single sip had been taken.

'No, we didn't in the end. The worst thing was she said she had over 500 contacts in there.'

Gu Lingzhou was taken aback. Had he really explained the whole ordeal as if it happened to someone else? Lao Han thrust the glass of beer back into Gu Lingzhou's hand, 'This sort of thing might be annoying, but it happens all the time. Who hasn't lost a phone before? People lose 'em every day.'

Gu Lingzhou sat silent, taking little, taciturn sips of his beer.

No matter how much everyone else kept pressuring him, Gu Lingzhou wasn't going to get drunk. He maintained his sobriety throughout the dinner, as if preserving a great deal of distance from Lao Han and the others, unable to lose himself in the festivities.

He remembered he had to make a few phone calls. First to his girlfriend – her number he knew. Then, suddenly, it struck him – should he give the woman from earlier a call? Amidst the raucousness of dinner, Gu Lingzhou began to reminisce about all the day's little minutiae, finally seeing clearly the cold, scintillating fangs behind fate's whimsical smile. Of all the warnings that had befallen him, that woman's call was without a doubt the most conspicuous... and he'd just abandoned her in that desolate place, night folding in from every corner, wrapping itself slowly around a handful of scattered houses, and in front of some squat little corner shop, beneath a burly, towering camphor tree, a woman waited, burning with anxiety.

By the time they left Fuyuan Inn, Lao Han and the others were already slurring their words in an unapologetically drunken haze. After he'd said his goodbyes, Gu Lingzhou hurried off to find a public phone booth into which he slipped a few coins to call his girlfriend. What if someone pretending to be him tried to scam her? OK, perhaps that was going a bit far. He had suspended his service already, and no one would have any way of making calls from his number. Tentatively, he dialled two numbers before pausing. He wanted to call the woman, but he'd forgotten the landline she'd called from. He'd always had a thing for numbers, and he'd had it memorised when he looked it up on his computer. Now, however, he was drawing a blank aside from the first two digits. Impatient, he randomly dialled a few more numbers, but they seemed totally off. Hanging up, he stood at a loss inside the phone booth.

In the Shanghai night, the phone booth seemed to Gu Lingzhou like a character, both deaf and mute. Whatever he wanted to tell it, it couldn't hear. Whatever it might want to tell him, it couldn't say.

All Gu Lingzhou could do was head back to the block of flats where he lived. Along the way, he passed a drab, fan-shaped plaza. Every evening, around nightfall, an earth-rumbling din of music would emanate from there, and hundreds of men and women would pair up, shimmying with an enthusiasm akin to primary school kids doing radio callisthenics in the morning before class. Most of the people were elderly, though some were middle-aged, and four or five children also darted in and out of the mass.

Most days, he'd zip right past the perimeter. He'd done it a thousand times before. He couldn't stand the gaudy music, not to mention the cloying movements and expressions of the men. Gu Lingzhou wasn't sure how he was managing to be standing there now. He looked on at them; the dim streetlamps illuminating a strange look of solemnity on their faces. Gu Lingzhou furrowed his brow, his expression as serious as those he was watching. He didn't know what he was thinking about. Then again, maybe he was thinking about nothing.

Then, the sound of a mobile ringing. Gu Lingzhou gave a start, reached out and began feeling around in his pockets. Empty. The ringing cut off, and another guy stood next to him, also spectating, took out his phone. Without realising it, Gu Lingzhou stood there gawking at the man, watching his lips wriggle, the blue light from his phone undulating in time to their movements. Noticing Gu Lingzhou staring at him, the man gave him a glower before turning around and heading off, as if afraid some secret might be overheard. Gu Lingzhou stood expressionless. Then he came too. What the hell was he doing here? All of a sudden, he was gripped by a sense of bemused incompleteness, and his feet began dragging him home, to the cheers of the dancing mass behind him. He didn't look back.

Dim lights dotted the apartment complex, a couple of people slipped past him on the pavement, now and then, but otherwise the street was quiet. Ordinarily, Gu Lingzhou would've headed straight for his flat, turned on his computer and logged into his email, Fetion, MSN and QQ to check if he had any messages. But without his phone, his main source of contact, there didn't seem much point checking these others. More than 500 numbers, and now, not one of these people could get in touch with him. He was like some crafty fish who'd slipped through a net woven from 500 cords. Was it a blessing? Or a curse? This net, though designed for ultimate convenience, had also proven impossibly fragile. Apparently, it was this easy for someone to disappear. Not a soul could find him now. The sense of bemused incompleteness tightened its grip. In his seven years using a mobile, he'd imagined this day coming, but never really believed it would arrive. Nothing was impossible, it turned out.

Gu Lingzhou opened up his backpack once again, turning it inside out. He'd already been forced to search through it so many times that day, he knew there was no way he'd find it now, but, just so, he picked through it with a fine-tooth comb one more time. Searching, it seemed, was of some small comfort. His earphones and battery pack were in there, but, inevitably, no trace of his phone. Once again, he faced up to the truth.

He walked right through the entrance to his building and into the empty space at the centre of the block – the courtyard. There was some exercise equipment there he'd used with his girlfriend when they first moved in. Out of habit, Gu Lingzhou walked over to a leg machine. He stepped up into the pedals and started moving his legs back and forth. He had looked up the name of this piece of equipment online. It had a daunting name: the 'Spacewalker'. He enjoyed the feeling of sort of walking on thin air, the machine creaking under his feet. Then he came to an abrupt halt. What was his girlfriend up to now, he thought. Was she texting him to ask if he missed her? Was she trying to phone him having not heard back? Was she panicking, not knowing what to think when she realised his service had been suspended? His imagination ran wild. Was she thinking he was messing around with some other girl? No, that made no sense. If he were, he'd just turn off his phone. Not suspend the number. Maybe she was thinking something had happened to him? Like a car accident. Something clicked. He started imagining he really had been in a car accident. On the way home from work he'd been hit by a car. Died. His phone had been busted, and there was no driver's license or other identification anywhere to be found to prove who he was. So, just like that, he vanished. He was frightened and dejected, just as if he'd been in a car accident...

…and not a single soul had the slightest idea that he'd gone.

And what of the woman who'd called him earlier? Had she also disappeared just like this? Gu Lingzhou began to identify with that woman. The question was: Did she actually know him, or not? He recounted their conversation. She hadn't said her name, but she clearly knew him – even entrusted her safety to him. It was he who'd forgotten who she was and thus made her feel abandoned, unwilling to even give her his name. Gu Lingzhou was dumbstruck. That's exactly how it had played out! And now, it was he who felt abandoned. He'd somehow forgotten the name of someone who placed such importance on him. He was in a state of turmoil, desperate to remember the landline number she'd called him from, but the more he wracked his brain, the dimmer his memory grew. What was he forgetting? When he first discovered he'd lost his phone, he was thrown into discord at the very idea that he had more than 500 people's numbers saved in there. It was anxiety-inducing. Thinking about it now, he was slightly overwhelmed; how could he have over 500 contacts? He could barely remember ten per cent of them. He'd forgotten so many! Just as they'd forgotten him.

A shrill little kid tottered up to him, babbling something. Gu Lingzhou smiled, and two people – one old, the other middle-aged – came over and pulled the child towards them, as if he might have smiled the boy right out of existence.

Gu Lingzhou was in unusually low spirits as he finally entered his flat. When he'd suspended his phone service, he'd decided to buy an identical model the following day and pick up a new SIM at China Mobile. He'd shoot out a few messages online and figured he could probably relocate 60–70 per cent of his contacts. He now felt strikingly wronged. Just like that, he'd vanished and was frustrated he couldn't see how others were reacting to his disappearance. Hadn't he heard a story about this once? You know, someone fakes their own death, then hides at the back of the funeral hall to see who comes to mourn him. Maybe, he should pretend there really had been a car accident. See who was really itching to get in touch with him. Maybe give it the next three days... After all, tomorrow was Friday. He didn't have any appointments, nor was he in the mood to go to work. There was no telling how many times that author who was always griping about his book covers, or his drinking buddies or his girlfriend, would phone him. He imagined what would be going through their minds when they called only to hear, 'The number you have dialled is not in service'. He couldn't help but crack a self-satisfied little smile. He was like the Invisible Man. He could see others, but no one else could see him.

There was an enormous temptation to open up the array of other communication channels available to him, but he had to control himself. His heart fluttered nervously, like a kid waiting for a teacher to announce exam results. Gu Lingzhou didn't log into email, Fetion, MSN or QQ, and he hadn't the slightest idea what else to do without his mobile. Life had suddenly become a vast, empty wilderness. He opened up the music folder on his computer and listened to a few songs, but he'd grown tired of them long ago. He tried to search online for a new movie, but none of them piqued his interest. So, he looked up a few he'd seen a bunch of times, only to squint at each one of them on the screen before quickly tiring of them as well.

Out of habit, Gu Lingzhou felt in his pocket for his phone, and for a split-second, it was as if he'd never lost it, as if it had all been a dream, and he was now waking up — his phone still cradled neatly in his pocket, those 500-plus people still there for him to contact or be contacted by. It didn't have to be a dream, he pondered. If time could just rewind a bit, if he could just be a bit more careful as it played forward again, he wouldn't have lost his phone. And he'd be safe now. Those 500-plus people would still be following him closely, and there'd be no way for him to disappear.

Gu Lingzhou's mood hit rock bottom. He feebly picked up a book on cover design and sprawled out on the bed to read before unintentionally drifting off. He had a chaotic mess of dreams. Not about his phone. Not about car accidents. He dreamed of a big lake filled with crystalline waters, yellow floating heart flowers abound. Without fully realising what he was doing, he drew a little boat and pushed off into the water. As he was taking in his surroundings, the boat suddenly vanished, and he quickly sank. He'd never realised he was so heavy. As he drifted downwards, he groped around in all directions, the tender floating heart stems slipping through his fingers. He awoke covered in sweat, screaming. He turned off the light, tossing and turning amid the blackness before falling asleep again.

Friday: his lost phone still occasionally crossed his mind.

Saturday: he felt that this was how life had always been.

Sunday: Gu Lingzhou woke at noon after a night of wild, tempestuous dreams. He only remembered the last dream before he woke up, but in it he called the woman. She was standing under a camphor tree like some slender, porcelain artefact still waiting for him. When he finally arrived, the camphor tree suddenly toppled over on top of her, scattering its leaves and branches across the ground. In a frenzy, he pried apart the branches, but the woman was nowhere to be seen. Instead, what he found was his phone.

Having decided to purchase a new phone that afternoon, Gu Lingzhou became elated. He never once considered getting a different phone or going to a different store. He even prepared himself. If the store didn't have that particular model in stock, he'd wait for them to order it in. Fortunately, he got the type he wanted without a hitch. The owner of the shop even remembered him. In no time, the ringtone and home screen had been switched back to precisely how they were with the original phone, and Gu Lingzhou was on his way to the China Mobile centre over in Wujiao Chang neighbourhood to replace his SIM. He inserted the card into his phone then inserted the phone into his pocket. He never thought it would be so simple.

With the buoyant air of a freshly charged electric scooter, Gu Linghzou went back home. With his phone restored, he would allow himself to turn on his computer, log into his email, Fetion, MSN, and QQ, and reconnect with the world outside. In an instant, the ropes that had snapped so precipitously were once again secured around him. Just the day before he thought he'd already grown accustomed to an empty life, and now, in an instant, he'd found that he rather preferred the incessant fetters of modern life. These binds made him feel truly alive, plugged into countless human connections. Unable to control himself, excitement seemed to well beneath his skin, bursting like little, white-hot sparks, so that when he turned his computer on, his hands were visibly shaking. He had survived three days in those desolate badlands just waiting to reap his harvest. But he couldn't put his finger on what exactly he thought people's inability to contact him would look like. Acrimony? Worry? Unease? Whatever it was, he'd revel in it. That was the truly marvellous thing – even if people reamed him out, he'd still feel delighted.

His computer didn't seem to share in his anticipation, chugging sluggishly along like always. It took everything he had not to lose it. When it finally booted up, he first opened his inbox. There were seven new emails – five from coworkers discussing business matters, and two that went to junk mail. Then he opened up QQ. Most of the blinking avatars were groups. Only two private messages to him. One from Lao Han asking if he'd been drunk the other night and one from a coworker asking if he'd revised a book cover or not. Then came Fetion and MSN. A pithy zilch from both.

It couldn't be.

Gu Lingzhou sat in front of his computer caught completely off guard, his brain brought momentarily to a halt. Stalled like a computer. He'd previously resolved to relish in other people's reactions to his absence. Instead, it seemed everyone else was stoically waiting for him to react. He took a deep breath. Could no one really have noticed his service had been shut off? Could no one have noticed something wasn't right with him these past three days? No, impossible. But right there as plain as could be, not a soul had asked why his phone had been cut off, they all thought it was normal that he hadn't responded to them immediately.

It was only now Gu Lingzhou realised that after getting his phone back, there wouldn't be a single call or text. He'd assumed that when he switched on his new phone, a slew of calls and texts would be waiting for him. Condemnation, suspicion and concern from his panicked girlfriend. Nitpicking and admonishment about book covers from the dissatisfied author...

But... it had all been in his head. From his phone to his computer, the lines were all so silent. His world was genuinely silent.

Unable to resist any longer, Gu Lingzhou finally called his girlfriend. Listening to the distant ring, he actually felt a bit nervous. Two rings. Three rings. His girlfriend wasn't picking up. Hadn't she been unable to contact him these past few days? What gives? Agitated, and mildly annoyed at himself for lying in limbo for three days, he dialled again. By his third dejected dial, the call was finally picked up, his girlfriend's voice carried through from far off.

'What's up? You miss me?' his girlfriend giggled.

Before Gu Lingzhou had a chance to answer, she cut in,

'Sorry to leave you hanging the past few days. I wasn't home two days before I got tied up with my friend. She was just begging me to go out. Its been a hectic three days. I've been falling asleep the moment I get to the hotel each night, so I haven't texted. Anyway, we're at the beach still, its super windy. It's tough to hear. Can you hear the wind? Listen!'

Gu Lingzhou could hear the wind, like a broom bushing across his eardrums.

'Do you miss me?' his girlfriend's voice came through surreal and unfamiliar in the murmur of the wind.

'I lost my phone,' he blurted.

'How?! How could you be so stupid?' Noticing his silence, she added, 'Whatever. Tons of people lose their phones. If it's lost, it's lost. Just get another and it's all good. But I'm guessing you've already got a new one anyway, right?'

'Yeah, I got another,' he said tepidly.

After a couple more mindless sentences of conversation, he hung up.

And so his girlfriend hadn't tried to reach him either. Gu Lingzhou gripped his phone like a melting ice cube. Who was there left to reach out to now? More than 500 strings of numbers. He couldn't remember all of them. He couldn't even find anyone to confirm that he'd lost his phone, to the point that he started questioning whether he'd ever truly lost it. The phone in his hand was still the same one he'd had... as far as appearances, at least, nothing had changed at all. A massive crack had fractured his life, and with the gentlest stroke, it had been filled evenly in. No one would know, and no one cared that this massive fissure had split apart his life. The day might even come when he himself would question whether such a rift had ever occurred in his otherwise smooth life. But, somewhere in the world, this sort of thing was happening all the time, people undauntedly facing the unanticipated, and adapting to it. Life was simply a case of using each ordinary today to neutralise another tomorrow. Time, in its frightening guise, cancelling out the disparities between one day and the next. Not only were other people unaware of the incongruities, the day may even come when the people concerned would doubt themselves. It was harrowing.

Preoccupied, Gu Lingzhou absent-mindedly pressed a couple of numbers on his phone pad, when suddenly the number of the strange woman bobbed right back up from the bottom of his memory in perfect sequence. He couldn't believe it at first, but kept backpedalling and plucking the numbers right out of his head. Though each digit was reassembled from a hazy starting point, this was the right number. He felt as though he was suddenly back on that office balcony, the number hovering right there behind his eyelids. Frantically he tapped in the digits and hit 'Call'.

It went through with a deee deee ring. It was dusk, and Gu Lingzhou was standing by his window, looking out over the gradually dimming apartment complex. A row of camphor trees lined the road adjacent, the warm radiance of the setting sun pastelled between their branches. He clenched his phone as if it were disintegrating right in front of him. This time, he was certain the woman knew him. Not only that, they were close. So close he didn't know why they'd ever lost touch. This was yet another rift in his life – one that he himself had filled in – and then he'd fooled himself it had never been there. Phone still ringing, it felt like a melting ice cube in his sweaty hand. Then, from the other end, came the languid rasp of a man's voice, half-scaring the life out of him.

'Hello?'

'Hello.'

'You are…?'

'I'm looking for…'

Gu Lingzhou was stupefied. *Who am I looking for? I don't even know who I'm looking for!* Furrowing his brow, he scrambled to think of how to describe the woman. 'I'm looking for a woman,' came his tentative reply.

'What?'

'Is this a… a corner shop? Don't you have a… a big… a big camphor tree out front?'

Gu Lingzhou stuttered, beads of sweat rapidly seeping from his forehead.

'Who on God's earth is this?' came the frustrated voice on the other end.

'Three days ago, a woman called me from your shop saying she'd lost her phone and wallet. I don't suppose she's still there?'

'What are you talking about?! No, there's no one like that here!' spouted a voice that went from alarmed to booming.

The call ended with a slam.

Gu Lingzhou wiped his brow. Why was he sweating so much? He waited a moment before calling again. The man hung up as soon as he heard his voice. Not to be discouraged, Gu Lingzhou rang again. No one picked up. He called again. Without so much as a hello, the man yelled, 'What the fuck's wrong with you?!' before slamming the phone down.

Standing dumbstruck in front of the window, Gu Lingzhou clutched his lubricious phone. It felt like it might slip out of his hand at any second. Gazing at the dusk-enshrouded apartment complex, vehicles passing back and forth in the distance, he knew if he didn't do something, this latest rift – the one with the woman – would also be mended, and soon he'd forget she ever existed. This time, however, he wasn't willing to let it happen.

He imagined himself donning his backpack, grabbing his keys and heading downstairs. At the entrance to the complex, he would hop on the bus and find a seat in the back by the window, watching as the familiarity of his neighbourhood slowly faded into the distance. The bus's movement would be punctuated by intermittent stops. He'd get off at the last stop and grab another bus to the suburbs, the skyscrapers shrinking closer and closer to the ground as he looked back at them, with trees springing up in their place. Vermillion oleander and red African arrowroot would line the road accompanied by vast fields. Real fields! There were fields in Shanghai. What might be growing in them in this season? They were on the heels of Mid-Autumn Festival and the rice harvest would be fast approaching back home. The land would be adorned in rich, creamy yellows. He wasn't sure if it would be rice-harvest season in Shanghai as well, but he was more than happy to imagine that was rice filling those fields. Thus, great swathes of golden rice sprawled out before his eyes, groups of farmers busy with the harvest, occasionally spooking flocks of birds into flight as they worked. Crows, perhaps? Pitch black, scattered in an instant across dusk's quiet horizon, like little black sesame seeds sprinkled atop a cool, celadon plate. The farmers would pause from their task at hand and gaze up at the birds, as Gu Lingzhou himself watched for a brief eternity before the feathered beings dove aslope into the lush branches of a camphor tree.

This was the camphor tree!

Gu Lingzhou was elated. He hopped off the bus before it could come to a complete stop, bounding straight for the camphor tree kicking up fresh dust as he went. After such a long journey, he was met by a village that he seemed to know from long ago, a camphor tree out front with the woman standing under it, looking up at him, waiting for him like a slender, porcelain artefact. He understood her. He knew it. And she understood him.

Gu Lingzhou, however, couldn't imagine what the second half of this scene would bring; all he could muster was the scene of him running toward the woman. The road between them seemed endless, and he was so weak, his legs felt like jelly. He imagined with all his might and he still couldn't make it to her. Moreover, it was dark now. The glow of the scant few streetlights was just enough to illuminate tiny plots beneath their respective poles. He couldn't even imagine the road he had been running down. Staring at the glass in front of him, the window gradually divulged a strange countenance. Unkempt hair. Protruding cheekbones. A dull gaze. Lips aslant. And a large, bulging nose. It brought to mind a line from some novel: 'He didn't like it when other people took note of his nose. It looked like a pupa, bound up in its hard shell.'

Notes

1. A suburban district of southwestern Shanghai, neighbouring Zhejiang province and Hangzhou Bay.
2. A renowned Taiwanese cartoonist, known for his signature use of vibrant colours and elaborately dressed characters.

Transparency

Xiao Bai

Translated by Katherine Tse

IT FELT LIKE BEING inside a cavernous, many-legged behemoth, that underground car park with its dense network of lanes. A suspect odour hung in the air. I stood next to Malin's Mini and pressed my face against the window, peering inside. After shadowing her husband home, I had planned on having noodles for dinner before going home to write up today's report. Then I had caught sight of Malin leaving the house and, on impulse, decided to follow her instead.

She was most likely in the gym upstairs, drenched in sweat. Her best friend had said that Malin struggled with anxiety and always carried fluoxetine. Drugs and exercise made an odd pair, if you ask me.

A Buick MPV drove past me, the hazy glow of two LED screens visible through the gap in the curtains. Nowadays, the streets were full of people in my trade, carrying on all sorts of dodgy business. That particular posse – so flashy and well-equipped – seemed to be rubbing shoulders with the right customers. I only had a few and relied entirely on word-of-mouth. I have no idea how they hear about me, though some of them might tell me, 'My friend Snowden mentioned you this one time…'

Malin had found me after her friend anonymously

emailed me. She wanted me to contact Malin because, 'Malin would never think of hiring you people herself,' but she also wanted to be kept out of it.

'She's too sensitive,' her friend said. 'They'll only fight at home.'

'What if she doesn't want to hire me?' I asked.

'Find a way. Tailor a couple of ads for her and have them pop-up on her desktop so that she keeps seeing it. Inundate her with the information. She'll contact you soon after.'

That wasn't hard. I just needed to touch up some templates I already had on hand and upload them to her server.

'She'll feel like it's more confidential if she finds you herself,' the friend added. 'I'll pay for it regardless.'

I did end up hearing from Malin, who paid me a deposit and officially hired me. Still, her friend would sporadically email me (I never DM my clients) and provide me with background information – 'just to save you the hassle'. She was even generous enough to pay me herself, on top of the payments I got from Malin.

Malin was just that kind of woman; people would do anything for her. If you ever met her, you'd understand why.

Malin had hired me to keep her husband under surveillance, but she had nothing conclusive on him, other than her doubts. Then again, she wanted those doubts erased. It was a thorny case. To prove that I wasn't just taking her money and skiving off, I gave her daily reports on her husband's comings and goings. Sometimes she responded enthusiastically, asking questions about all the vague parts of the report. At other times, when she was in a noticeably low mood, she would berate me for taking her money and patching together this arbitrary timetable in the evening.

Just as I was about to propose quitting the case, Malin invited me out. I rarely met with my clients in person. To some degree, I saw my work as a strictly online business.

But I went. That night, her friend emailed me and asked, 'What happened? Have you promised her you'll stay on?'

'How did you know? Did she say something to you?'

'Course not. She doesn't know about me. What do you think about her?'

'She's a looker.'

'Not that. I mean, do you think she's all right? Why do I feel like she's always so highly strung?'

As soon as she said that, I started thinking that maybe Malin did have some mental health issues. Her husband was a workaholic. I had specifically asked my uncle about him – my uncle Xu Xiangbei. You've probably heard his name. He treats me like a son. I know nothing about my father, except that he was called Xu Xiangbi. Whenever my uncle and aunt spoke of him, it was always in hushed tones.

My uncle said to me, 'Xiaotong, do you remember a card game called "Pack of Lies"? We would always play that when you were young. That game's a bit like your line of work.' I had used that same metaphor with Xiaohua. That was Malin's friend – she had let slip her name in one of our emails.

Speaking of my 'line of work', the methods in this trade have changed completely over recent years. We no longer tail people or search through rubbish bins, nor do we have to navigate our way around different types of locks. Nowadays, we fish around; we intercept people's correspondence. We stay at home, reluctant to get our hands dirty. We don't even want to meet clients face-to-face because, technically speaking, their cases have nothing to do with us. With Malin, though, I had started breaking some of my own rules.

Missteps can happen. I once heard about a highly skilled thief who had meant to burgle a home. He had the target confirmed and every step plotted. He pried open the door, switched off the lights – and tripped over a Russian Blue cat, which so enamoured him that he forgot his plan altogether. In the end, he was caught.

Maybe I liked the view from behind. Maybe you would too, if you spent all your time following her, watching her move gracefully around in her soft, tailored clothing.

There was once a short story about a psychiatrist who fell in love with a female mental health patient and it ended up ruining his life. But thoughts like that in terms of me and Malin – well, people like me tend to get a little delusional, and anyway, it's all harmless.

Or maybe I should rephrase that and say I'm fascinated by Malin and her husband.

I usually have no desire to get to know the client any better. It would only make things more difficult.

The other night, I had started coding and wrote:
header(content-type:image/png);......

It produced a tracking pixel with a linker script, which showed up as a transparent image. I inserted it into an email and saved it as a draft. If my recipient ever opened the email, the pixel would feed the data back to the server – and to me.

I held back for a few days. Clearly, I had my reservations. After all, if someone was willing to pay for this, why did I need to confirm *their* identity?

Back in the car park, I peeled myself away from Malin's Mini and sent off the email.

Then I drove my Mazda to buy a pizza and remotely logged into the server from my laptop. Two slices later, I started playing a round of PlayerUnknown's Battlegrounds, choosing a sniper rifle as my weapon, and mulled over the case.

The server set up in their house pinged: Xiaohua had opened my email on her phone. She had yet to reply, though. Usually she had an answer for everything, but maybe she was treading lightly. After all, the data from the tracking pixel had her pinned at Malin's home right now, while Malin herself was out. Maybe Xiaohua was too preoccupied to check her email.

I had had an inkling that there was more to this case, and now the evidence was clear. People who cared far too much usually had their own motives. It left a bad taste in my mouth, even if they had booked a hotel to do the deed.

I parked next to Malin's Mini and strode decisively to the elevator. In the gym upstairs, Malin was on the rowing machine. It had been 15 minutes, and as expected, she still hadn't finished her 2,000 strokes.

She seemed surprised to see me. My message hadn't gotten to her.

Now was the moment. I always had some hesitations, but the timing was probably right. Having just worked out, she was feeling a little more relaxed, a little more detached.

'You'll never guess who the other woman is,' I said without preamble. Best to skip the niceties, just as you would with criticism.

She looked at me, bewildered. 'Who are you talking about?' she asked, slowly unbuckling her foot straps.

'Xiaohua. Do you consider her your best friend?'

She shook her head.

'Maybe you don't think so, but that's what she told me.' This woman didn't even want to hear the truth, I thought.

'Your best friend – she's at your house right now,' I continued. 'You weren't wrong to suspect your husband. The problem was with your friend. Your best friend.'

Suddenly she burst into laughter, spasming uncontrollably as sweat dripped from her hair. If she was any less attractive, I'd have thought her a madwoman. Even so, I still think she was a bit crazy.

She said she was going to change and told me to carry on the investigation until I had evidence. She would keep paying me by the hour, regardless of the outcome.

Then, to my surprise, Xiaohua emailed and asked to meet at a café. She technically had no reason to contact me, but given the state of affairs right now, she had become my client too, in some twisted way. I had no reason not to go.

I braced myself, ready to reject her at every turn. In my mind, she was nothing but a scheming woman.

She never came, but Malin's husband did. The man himself, finally.

'Xiaohua invited me. Why are *you* here?' I asked pointedly, trying to needle him.

Unruffled, he ordered a double espresso. Then he made a business call and checked his messages, even as I sat there waiting. Finally –

'There never was a Xiaohua,' he said. 'That was me.'

What an idiot I was! 'Helping Malin hire someone to investigate yourself? Smart.' I added knowingly, 'Hiding a secret in plain sight. A directory for storing personal photos –'

'I don't have a secret life,' he interjected. 'I hardly have a life. That's what she has a problem with.'

As soon as he said that, he rapped his knuckles against his temples. His voice abruptly dropped to a mumble, as if he suddenly needed to catch his breath. Perhaps he regretted saying that to an outsider.

He gulped down the espresso and said that he should've been honest from the start. Malin had given him hell until, at last, she had furiously brought up the name 'Xiaohua'. As soon as he heard, he knew that it was time to come clean.

'Sometimes she pushes me so far that I want to get a divorce,' he said, 'but we married right after college, and I just don't have the heart for it.' Then he had struck upon an idea: if he had an informant keeping an eye on him for Malin, everything about him would be completely transparent to her. 'Maybe she would get off my back if she knew what I did every day,' he explained.

Per his request, I continued to send Malin daily reports, though I now felt differently about them. Each report became a creative work of literature, each sentence crafted with painstaking care, in the hope that it might sway its reader. Men and women nowadays — what a tangled web they weave.

When I told my uncle this story, he mused, 'I bet he can't get a divorce. If they married right after college, he probably didn't have much money at the time and didn't sign a prenup. Maybe his wife owns a part of their company. They don't have huge profits in that line of business, and their finances are all quite transparent. It's possible that if he ever tried to leave her, their company could collapse.'

His words only made me more suspicious. Now, a little while later, I can't help but think that maybe, just maybe, Malin had known all along.

Suzhou River

Cai Jun

Translated by Frances Nichol

It was afternoon, and I could feel my forehead and hair warming in the rays of the sun. The light had snuck into my room, and into me. Exhaling lightly, I eventually opened my eyes. I had no idea what I'd been doing lying on the bed, with the sunlight forcing my eyelids open, dazzling me.

Where was I?

I looked at the high ceiling and the blue and white walls. Set in one of them was a balcony, and through its glass windows, the sun's rays created a languorous atmosphere that enveloped me, making me drowsy. Eventually I stood up and began pacing back and forth. The room felt unfamiliar. In the floor-length mirror on one wall, I caught sight of a mocking face. Seeing myself marching backwards and forwards, I felt suddenly disorientated. Then I noticed the letter on the desk.

Yes, that letter. Light was spilling onto the desk and the letter reflected it, blindingly. Bending down, I saw that it was written on some kind of special paper. It looked like Duoyunxuan brand writing paper, but on further inspection, it wasn't. I picked it up gently. Still in the sun, the glossy surface of the paper shone brightly, its white light making everything swim. It took my eyes a moment to adjust before

I could gradually begin to make out the characters on the page...

> My C,
> I received your letter yesterday afternoon. I'm so sorry. It was out of the blue, and at first, I wanted to ignore it. But it seems I do have a faint memory of you. Yesterday evening I was bored and had basically nothing to do all night. And when I was by the window looking at the moonlight, I suddenly remembered what you look like. Yes, it was you. Every morning, you walk past, below my building, and occasionally you wave hello. But you never say anything. Maybe you won't believe it, but I do remember your melancholy eyes. I just hope I haven't remembered your name wrong.
> C, you might not believe this either, but just now, when I was bored, I somehow ended up pulling out a map of Shanghai. I find it hard to understand why people would come here from all over the world to build a city this big, when all I need is a little flat. No, don't come to my home looking for me. As you know, there's a river that flows through the centre of the city, and there are quite a few bridges crossing it. I like bridges. I trust you do too. So, let's meet this evening at 6 o'clock and I'll wait on the bridge that you cross every morning.
> Your Z.
> Early morning, 16 December
> xxxx

This was clearly a letter to me from the woman. It was the first time I had seen her handwriting and it was much like I had imagined. Holding the letter, I could still detect a faint fragrance radiating from the paper. Perhaps it was a special incense she used in her room or on her body. I took a deep greedy breath through my nose so the fragrance quickly filled my chest. Where did this paper come from? For some reason, I had just been napping. I felt confused. I had to think a while before I could find the vague memory that this morning, a child delivered a letter to my door. What did the child look like? Where did they come from? I couldn't remember. It was as if it never happened, except this piece of paper and these words were in my hands.

'Z'. She called herself Z. The last letter of the alphabet. Maybe it had a special significance? Or was it just a coincidence? Like how she called me 'C'. But I had another question now. Did I write a letter? Maybe I did. Maybe I didn't. Did I write a letter to her? Maybe it was her. Maybe it wasn't. What I was sure of, now, was that I should – no, I had to – stroll over the bridge at the time specified. The 16th – today – at 6 in the evening. It was a suggestive time, filled with unlimited possibility.

I opened the glass doors to the balcony and leaned against the railings. The balcony protruded from the building like the defensive bastion of a city wall. The railings, made of iron, curled in a pattern at the corners. Honestly, I liked my balcony. I often sat there to read, in the lazy sun, the wind blowing in all directions, lightly brushing my forehead and the pages of the book. I lived in a six-floor building with dark walls and European-style ornaments. From my second-floor balcony, I looked across the street. The north/south-running road beneath was so narrow I could see almost everything that went on in the glass-fronted offices opposite. Instead, I turned to look northeast, towards buildings of various shapes and styles built by Europeans. Of the many windows either tightly closed or flung wide open, I knew one was Z's. But I couldn't see her, so I cast my gaze beyond to the furthest thing I could see, the arse of the Bund. I call those tall buildings the arse of the Bund because I look at them from behind. That's the perspective I'm used to.

I left the balcony and headed into another room, to the left of the narrow bedroom: my bathroom. I didn't have much of value, except in my bathroom. There, I had something that was the envy of many: a large, pure-white steel bathtub. In the bathroom, I brushed my teeth, washed my face, and quickly shaved my beard. Then I changed into new clothes and left the flat.

The lift for my block of flats made a whirring noise whenever it moved. I stepped inside and pulled the folding door shut. Next, the lift machinery sounded and the steel chains above my head slowly pulled up, lowering me down. Through the doors I saw the second floor slowly rise and the corridor of the first floor come into view, then the downstairs lobby. I opened the doors again with some effort. The lobby was always dirty and chaotic so I quickly passed through and out onto the street.

The sun was just about managing to penetrate between the surrounding buildings, sliced into thin strips that fell on the road and streaked across my face. I took a deep breath and thought how the narrow road squeezed between the two tall rows of buildings looked like a deep mountain valley. I made it to the junction quickly. The road here was even more crowded. Looking up at the two rows of buildings in a mishmash of styles, I felt like I'd walked into a giant labyrinth. This was the right metaphor. The city actually is a giant labyrinth. The outer roads are spacious and wide, but if you come closer into the centre, over here, they are denser, narrower and windier. You can never see to the end of the street. Instead, you face constant forks in the roads and dead ends, or you find yourself going round and round in circles. They say that some people who come here never find their way out again. Like this European walking past. His face is pale and he's tall, but extremely thin. He looks weak enough to be taken down by a gust of wind. I've seen him countless times before. He passes me silently, always going in the same direction. Sometimes I see him at dusk, and other times at dawn. No-one knows his destination. Maybe his goal is to find his destination. But he can't find it, and never will, because he's lost. So he keeps walking the same streets, day after day, year after year. He's already a slave to this giant labyrinth. Actually, sometimes I am too.

After my brush with the poor European, I suddenly asked myself: Where am I going? I re-read the letter Z sent me in my head. The bridge. I knew that bridge. I crossed it every morning. It has a large steel frame on top, and a deck covered with cement and asphalt. From afar, it looks like an iron net has been erected above the water. The bridge rose up in my vision, spanning my path, and the road beneath my feet morphed into a muddy river.

I'd already crossed multiple junctions. The buildings around me now were all dark grey and hemmed me in from all sides. At the entrance to one tower, I saw an Indian man, maybe a Sikh, with dark skin and a large beard. His head was wrapped in a red turban. He was dignified, guarding the entrance, at work. I took a few more steps and suddenly heard the melodious rising and falling tones of a bell. It was the sound of the Custom House bell. It often woke me early in the morning, but I was fond of it. The bell had a steamy tang, reminiscent of the fog that gathers along the river banks at dawn.

I couldn't go any further ahead, so I crossed the narrow road and turned into a small lane between two black buildings. I'd actually never been through there before, but I had a feeling it could be a shortcut. What I didn't know was that a lot of people lived down there, between these two huge buildings. Wearing worn-out clothes, they went about their business: scrubbing bedpans, squatting with toddlers and encouraging them to wee, playing mah-jong. Yet they didn't seem to care about my incursion. The sides of the buildings were so high that the ground beneath probably never saw the sun at any time of year. I looked up at the sky. There was only a thin sliver left, from which a bright white light quietly fell. As I walked further inside, the alley narrowed until only one person could pass at a time. Suddenly, the light dimmed completely. The buildings joined together above my head and I entered a sort of tunnel. The narrow passageway made me feel like I'd entered someone's house: other people were living their lives just inches above my head. I heard a burst of screams and a gang of boys squeezed past me, forcing me to turn sideways and press against someone's wall while their boisterous noise faded away. Looking ahead, all I could make out was a small spot of light, seemingly suspended mid-air.

I finally made it out of the under-passage. Blocking my way ahead was another narrow road, but on the other side was the embankment of the Suzhou River. I inhaled greedily, and the sunlight suddenly felt brighter than ever before. I thought that I should take a look at the river before I went to the bridge. Crossing the road, I saw an older lady on a small wooden stool bathing in the sun. Her face was heavily wrinkled but she looked content, as if she were soaking in a bath of sunlight itself. A strange thought flashed through my mind: This is probably what Z will look like a few decades from now.

I climbed the embankment and leaned over the concrete railings to look at the turbid water. The sun cast a golden shimmer across the surface of the broad river, concealing its original colour. The river runs west to east and flows very gently. Today, its surface was extraordinarily calm, with just a few ripples softly disturbing the brilliant sunlight. The reflection on the surface looked like countless mirrors smashed into fragments and pieced together again. The broken, gilded reflections pierced my eyes like shards of glass. But suddenly, something about the calm Suzhou River felt off. The usual endless parade of wooden and iron boats, solitary steamers and slow-moving barges tugged in rows like train carriages: where was it? Had the boats followed the current out into the Huangpu? Or had they gone upstream to dock alongside the fields fragrant with mud on the outskirts of the city? The river was lonely without its ships, I was sure of that.

It was high tide. I didn't know if it was water flowing back in from the Huangpu River or the branches joining the northern bank, or if it was simply the pull of the moon, but I noticed the river slowly starting to rise. Maybe the river bed had become higher due to the accumulation of sediment and rubbish over the years, but the amount the river was rising surprised me, because this was the dry season. I watched the waterline steadily climb the opposite bank and immerse the parts that had always been dry. Still it showed no sign of stopping. Gradually, the water reached as high as the surface of the road on the other side of the embankment, and then continued to rise, still covered in a sparkling gold. I suddenly realised that the embankments would not hold it back. Sure enough, just a few minutes later, the river had risen to just a few inches below the concrete railing. It occurred to me that if I stretched my hands down, I could easily wash them in the Suzhou River's muddy waters. It reminded me of my big bathtub at home, full of water and ready for me to climb in. Now was the time for me to reach my hand down to test the temperature.

But I didn't want to bathe in the Suzhou River.

I quickly left the railing and jumped down from the embankment. The old lady enjoying the sun had disappeared. Maybe she'd had a premonition. I crossed the road. Not wanting to go back into that lightless tunnel beneath the buildings, I hurried in another direction. Suddenly, I heard a sound behind me. The same sound as when my bathtub is full, and I sit down into it, and the water slowly flows over the rim. I looked back to find that the Suzhou River had now climbed to the highest point of the bank, its water slowly spilling over the concrete railings and soaking the ground. Actually, it was more like a waterfall. A long, dark – or rather, due to the sun, seemingly golden – waterfall, cascading over the wide stretch of railing. The water brimmed over the embankment and poured onto the road the embankment was meant to protect. The Suzhou River was spreading wantonly across once dry streets. I had to get out of there. I quickly walked to the junction and then hurried south. A few steps later, I looked back. Now it was as if a full bathtub had suddenly been toppled over. The water was coursing over the road.

Rivers have their own way of being. They're gentle, yet powerful. Calm, but passionate. Now, I was watching the Suzhou River overflowing with passion. It was expansive, rampaging through the streets, beyond its embankments. I said before that this city is like a giant labyrinth, and that countless streets join the road along the river. The difference between people and rivers, though, is that a person can only take one road at a time, while a surging river can rush along countless streets at the same time. A labyrinth presents endless possibilities, and only the river can finally make its way out.

The racing current was already knee-high in the streets along the bank. When the forward charge of the water reached a junction, it simply divided forces and flowed further into the city. That's the nature of water.

When I turned the corner onto a small north/south-running road, I discovered that the Suzhou River was now behind me, chasing me – maybe because I was an eyewitness to the water's rise. I didn't want to be taken captive by the river, so I ran away from its source. But it surged in close pursuit, never more than a few steps behind. I couldn't outrun the river, and eventually it caught up with me My shoes got wet. My socks and trouser legs too. It wasn't sunny anymore and I finally saw the true colours of the Suzhou River. Those were new trousers that the filthy water had soaked. I looked all around me in panic. Nearly all of the roads were now invaded by the deluge. The freezing water was almost at my shins, making me shiver. My whole body was ice-cold. I urgently needed to get home, back to my comfortable flat and, ideally, into the warmth of my coveted bathtub.

I ran in the direction of home, the tall buildings still looming high on either side of the narrow street. What before had resembled a valley, now looked like a muddy river gorge. I crossed junction after junction. Each one had become a small wharf where the river converged before flowing off in new directions. The water covered my thighs and would soon be at my waist. I really didn't want to have to swim down the street. Suddenly, I saw the Indian doorman. He was standing like a statue, still guarding the entrance of the building. His bottom half was completely submerged in the muddy water, and yet his top half could have been in the middle of the arid deserts of western India. I wanted to beckon him to flee with me, but I was scared I would be rebuffed. Nobody can tell him to move except his master. I had to leave him and get myself home.

The river water had risen to chest-height by this point. I eventually ran inside – or rather, swam inside – my building. I couldn't take the lift, so I made for the stairs. I ran up to the second floor without stopping, finally extracting myself from the river. After dragging my wet body into the flat, I peeled off all my clothes to prevent the filthy river water messing up my home and made a beeline to the bathroom. I have already mentioned my impressive bathtub. I filled it with steaming water and slipped into the piping heat. Having been soaked in the Suzhou River, and left trembling with cold, the hot waters of the bath were my only option.

Steam quickly enveloped the bathroom. My whole body was now submerged in the hot water, with only my head exposed. I shut my eyes to enjoy it, what had just happened almost forgotten. I would have liked to dream, but I didn't sleep in the end. Half-asleep, half-awake, I suddenly remembered Z.

How could I have forgotten about her? Z and I had agreed to meet at 6 o'clock on the bridge. I couldn't be late. But, there had been an incident. The Suzhou River had shut off all the roads, and I couldn't possibly swim to our date (and of course, more to the point, neither could she). But I guessed she didn't need me to tell her that. Maybe I should have phoned her to re-arrange. But I didn't know her number. Anyway, it didn't matter.

I was still in the bath, soaking in these daydreams, when a blast of cold air suddenly hit my back. The bathroom door was open. I looked at my flat from the bathtub. Incredible: it was full of water. Muddy water. Water from my bath? No. A split second later, I realised that this was the water of the Suzhou River.

Evidently, the river had risen much more than I expected, as high as the second floor. Sitting in the bathtub, I felt completely at sea. The river had spread to the edges of my tub and I was naked and helpless in the face of this reality. I removed the plug from the bottom of the bath so all the hot water drained out, and then immediately replaced it tightly over the hole. I knew what was going to happen next. The steel tub was not fixed in place with cement, just connected to a drain. Before long, I noticed that the bathtub was starting to float. The bathroom was already full of the turbid water, and the buoyancy of the tub was starting to lift it. There wasn't a drop of water in my bath now, only me, naked and alone. Looking at the rising water, I resigned myself to my fate.

Afloat, my bathtub carried me out of the bathroom and into my bedroom. It too was full of river water, of course, and some of the wooden furniture was starting to rise with it. I noticed a thick cotton-padded coat hanging on the wall, still dry above the water, and immediately reached out to grab it and wrap it tightly around myself to keep out the cold. Now bundled in the coat, I looked out the window. The flood had reached the level of the windowsill, and the building opposite was in a similar state. From here, it looked like I was in one of those canal-side towns to the south of the Yangtze. My bathtub had become a life raft with no motor. It carried me out of my flat to the balcony, although I couldn't actually see the balcony anymore. The water was too muddy: the iron railings were completely submerged and I couldn't make out a thing beneath me. The bathtub continued to drift out and I suddenly realised that if this had been a few hours earlier, I'd have been suspended high in the air right now. The junction three floors below me had already become a river bed. I imagined that river weeds were probably starting to take root even now, and that a deep current had already established itself between the two rows of buildings.

I lay back in my tub, helpless. I couldn't figure out if I was actually floating on water or flying through the air. All I could do was hold on tight to my coat collar and make sure I was wrapped up enough to stop the icy wind penetrating through to my naked body. The bathtub carried me downstream. Those dark towers still lined the banks, firm and immobile. Familiar roads had become rivers, but they were still dense and confusing. These rivers were like a labyrinth too, forever branching off and turning into dead ends. I thought I had better find an oar so I could row the bathtub like a boat and control where I was going. I had

141

always wanted to row a boat by myself along the web of canals to the south of the Yangtze and listen to the sound of the women's singing through the mist as they picked water chestnuts. But I never wished to find myself navigating naked in a steel bathtub, wrapped only in a padded coat. Yet I had no choice. Shivering, I surveyed the city all around me, submerged up to the second floor in this great deluge of water. I suddenly thought of the Indian doorman – no, the Sikh – probably still guarding the door at the bottom of the river. For some reason, I began to envy him.

All of a sudden, I noticed someone swimming by my tub. It turned out to be the European from before, the one who's lost, forever repeating himself, going round and round in circles, on a never-ending loop. He was still trying to find his destination even now, only this time he had to swim there. His technique actually looked very good. He swept past me again, silently, as before. But this time, I think I was more embarrassed than him.

My bathtub continued floating. I suddenly felt like I was lying in a cradle, in the embrace of the river, being rocked. Where would it take me?

I couldn't see the city clearly anymore. The labyrinth-like roads – no, rivers – kept criss-crossing, reproducing themselves. The endless walls of towers passed me by. It was as if I were on a river in the deepest rainforests of the Amazon. The only difference was, the sun had gone, and the cold winds of December were whistling bleakly past. Eventually, I began to tire. I pulled the coat tighter around me and slowly closed my eyes...

I don't know how long had passed, but when I opened my eyes again, I seemed to remember having floated across a vast sea. My mind was hazy, in a thick fog.

I looked around and discovered that I was no longer

flanked by tall buildings. Instead, I saw two long river banks. Where was I?

The Suzhou River.

Yes, I was on the Suzhou River. Or, to be more exact, the bathtub carrying me was on the Suzhou River. There was already no sign of the flood. Only the river remained, neatly trapped in its bed by the two embankments. The Suzhou River is very low during the dry season, at least three or four metres below the tops of the levees. At these times, you can even see the gravel of the river bed protruding above the water along the banks. The flood had receded, leaving as quickly as it had come. The absurd deluge had only lasted two or three hours, rapidly rising to the second floor and then just as rapidly reverting back to its dry season state, while my bathtub and I had been swept from the submerged streets onto the course of the river. It was a pity that when the flood retreated, it left me and my bathtub adrift down here. I yearned for a barge to trundle by so I could beg the North Suzhou-accented captain to pass me a bamboo pole and pull me along, or give me hot water to drink. But there weren't any boats about. Maybe they'd all been swept away by the flood, my bathtub the only one left.

The day was drawing in and the busy city was acting like nothing had happened. It was just another dusk. Neon lights flickered, emitting a dazzling brightness. Not a single trace was left of the devastating flood. I looked at the sleepless city, and then back at myself, pitiful, alone, floating on the current in the middle of the Suzhou River. But actually, I had a flat of my own, and a great balcony. And most importantly, I had a pure white steel bathtub where I could bathe in hot water. Today, it even saved my life. But could I even get back to my flat and balcony? Drifting along, my heart suddenly filled with despair and tears spilled weakly from my eyes. Perhaps I really was a weak person. But right now, I was cold. Cold enough to freeze, to really freeze. I was afraid I wouldn't be able to bear it much longer and would impulsively pull the plug out from the bath. Within 30 seconds, I would sink to the bottom of the Suzhou River.

What time was it? The question came to me suddenly. Naked, with nothing except this bathtub and the cotton-padded coat that covered me, I had no way to tell the time. It made me anxious.

Suddenly, from the direction of the Bund, came the sound of a huge clock. That's it: the Custom House clock. My god, how I loved this bell now. I counted silently: one… two… three… four… five… six. The melodious bells tolled six times. I looked at the darkening sky and the bright moon, slowly rising. It was six o'clock. *As the moon rises above the willow, there after dusk we meet.* I suddenly remembered my Z.

The bathtub continued to carry me down the river until suddenly, I saw a bridge ahead of me. I knew that bridge. The tall steel truss stood proud on top, its interlocking steel bars facing me like a web. I wrapped my coat tighter around me and carefully scanned the bridge as the current drew me closer. There was a woman in a coat standing by the iron railings. The streetlights along the bridge were pale but provided enough light for me to clearly make out her face from below, on the Suzhou River.

It was Z, my Z. Yes, it was her. She seemed to be about thirty years old – seven or eight years older than me. She had mid-length, slightly curly hair that fell childishly over her ears. She was lightly made up, and under the streetlight, I could see that she seemed to be waiting for someone. She kept looking south of the bridge.

She hadn't broken her promise. But neither had I. We both arrived at the bridge at the agreed time. The only difference was, she was on top of the bridge, and I was floating beneath it, protected from the elements only by a cotton-padded coat. I wanted to shout 'Good evening!' up to the bridge. But when she discovered a white steel bathtub floating on the Suzhou River, and that the bathtub held a man curled up in a coat, how would she react? I didn't dare think, let alone make a noise.

Suddenly, I noticed that a man had arrived on the bridge. He seemed very young and was wearing clothes I'd never seen before. He walked up to Z as if he knew her. She turned to him, smiling. Yet he seemed a little bashful, like me. Z's eyes flashed warmly under the streetlights. It should have been a look she gave me, but she gave it to this stranger. Naturally, I felt disappointed.

A gust of cold air blew over and I could suddenly hear their conversation on the bridge. The Suzhou River had pulled me to within five or six metres of it. It was a miracle I could hear them speak. In fact, everything I experienced that day was a miracle. I heard Z say to the man: 'Hello. So, it turns out you like to be on time.'

The man spoke in a quiet voice, a little timidly. Stammering, he said: 'I was really happy to get your letter. Why did you want to meet me on the bridge?'

Did Z write two letters? One to me, and the other to him? I started to lose hope.

Z said slowly: 'I wrote that because I remembered the sad look on your face, and I like this bridge and the Suzhou River.'

The young man seemed to hesitate, and then said: 'Let me tell you a strange story. Today, after I got your letter, I took a nap and had a strange dream. I dreamt that I was coming to find you, and I passed through all these old streets from decades ago. I came to the banks of the Suzhou River, and found it was suddenly rising. Eventually, it overflowed its banks and spilled onto the streets, turning into a heavy flood. I had to run home and, because I was soaked through, I took a bath. But, the water somehow came into my flat up on the second floor. And the bathtub started to float with me still in it. I sat in the bath, and I only had a padded coat to wrap myself in. I floated out of my block of flats and along the streets all submerged in the Suzhou River. Later on, I don't know how long, the water receded and I ended up floating in the bath in the Suzhou River. And everything had returned to normal, except I was still in the bath, drifting on the river. Then I woke up, scared and in a cold sweat. It was very odd.'

I listened to the conversation on the bridge, shocked. I looked up to try to see the face of the man. In the faint streetlight, I finally made it out. It was my face.

I trembled all over, and watched as Z and 'I' left the cold railings of the bridge. They walked close together, towards the south and the ever-hedonistic lights of the city.

Now the bridge was empty. Only I remained, in my bathtub, gently floating.

Wrapped in my cotton-padded coat, gently rocked by the ripples of the Suzhou River in the soft evening light, I finally slept. I dreamt that I floated out into the Huangpu River, then further out to the mouth of the Yangtze, and then out to the sea. Forever floating, until the ends of the earth.

State of Trance

Chen Qiufan

Translated by Josh Stenberg

SOME THINGS ANNOY YOU. It's as if human history is being kept from starting a new chapter; you know that the next page is totally blank, just like tonight – the last night on the planet. You decide to take action, an action that will place a perfect full stop at the end of civilisation.

You decide to go to Shanghai Library and return the book.

So is the library still there? The last thing you heard was that a bunch of savages from the university district, Wujiaochang, had charged into the stacks, but no, they didn't steal any valuable manuscripts or set fire to the place, it was just that they'd been repressed too long by knowledge's tomb-like hierarchy. They ate those books, literally ate them. You can't imagine what it would feel like to chew *Precis of Confucian Economics* up, slobbering, much the same way you can't grasp why there are people who love anything that smacks of durian.

At least the automated book return machine should still be there. Hopefully they haven't destroyed it, thinking it a vending machine.

You leave the little nest where you've been curled up so long, where water and food are ample – at the beginning, people used to fight for it, before realising how pointless that was. There's no time left, everything is void. The kitty emerges in a fuzzy confusion from its dream, meows indolently, looks at you, incomprehension manifest in its very whiskers. You envy all these creatures for whom self-consciousness has never transpired, though perhaps that doesn't even include the cat sitting here before you, for though it turns a blind eye to itself in the mirror, it is evidently aware that you are waving at it in the light's reflection. Perhaps the cat is simply too arrogant.

The alleys and streets don't seem to have changed at all, besides the mountains of garbage which no one clears away, although you don't smell the stench you would have expected. Perhaps the olfactory system too has collapsed, just as memory is gradually being effaced. They are all parts of the brain, but the scientists haven't figured out how the two are associated, and neither the madeleines nor the spring onion noodles matter one iota anymore.

You've never figured out what kind of person you are, what kind of life you'd like to live, just like every other human.

Unimportant.

A deafening sound flashes past you like lightning, filling the air with flying rubbish, like confetti at Greenwich's terminal moment – a motorcyclist screeching past like a knight of steel who prefers to die from a shot of adrenaline straight to the heart.

The guardians of order have all disappeared, or you could say that they have deconstructed themselves.

That's because the threat hasn't come from outside, like in the science-fiction movies, with aliens, or meteors, black holes, the reversal of the planetary axis, or else a sudden ice age, a plague, or Thanos, or whatever.

It's not like that. The most lethal threats often come from

the self, something that constitutes you, something you were once very proud of, rationality, emotion, love, humanity, or whatever.

Just like an iceberg, the part that begins to melt is beneath the surface, and by the time you hear the cracking, it will already be too late.

You cross through the iAPM mall at ground level, you don't know why you would want to, perhaps it's those shiny facades and brands that used to provoke your desire to consume, or perhaps you just want to take a look at the Moncler poster at the entrance, the artist Liu Bolin imitating an iceberg, though the poles no longer exist.[1]

A gigantic exhibition hall for materialism, in every detail revealing humanity's self-regarding nature, you tread on the shards of glass and look across the six-storey space, lifting up like a spaceship toward the universe, gazing deeply back at you like a black hole, while the ambient tracks of the shops intertwine in your memory, looping over and over again, like someone calling your name.

Yet you can't remember your name.

You can finally feel your hand's gravity, you see the book, with difficulty you make out the words on the cover: *Brain Entropy: A Theory of Neurocognition*. You don't even know why you would have borrowed a book like that. Is it so that you can figure out what's going on with the world, or maybe what's going on with yourself?

Not that you ever finished it. Just like you never finished the previous novel, about Shanghai – *The Diamond Age*. You always figured it was because of cell phones and the internet.

Now you know that wasn't so.

Cell phones and internet belong to history now, they can never again distract your attention like they did in the past, since your attention is just like the filling of a custard bun, it spills oouuuttttttt–

You eagerly open a page at random, you have to prove it to yourself, prove to yourself that you haven't entirely lost human self-respect.

The phenomenon of self-organised criticality refers to how complex systems are forced out of balance by regular energy inputs, so that once they reach a critical point in relatively narrow transition zones between systematic order and chaos, they begin to show intriguing characteristics: 1) a maximum number of metastable or transiently stable states 2) a maximum sensitivity to disturbance and 3) a tendency for cascade processes that tend to be disseminated throughout the system, known as 'avalanches'.

Reading the final word, you are satisfied; these symbols cannot provoke any meaningful reaction in your brain. They appear randomly, like one black bird after another, internally unconnected, just colliding with another, scattering feathers all over the ground.

The human brain is precisely such a complex system.

You lift your head out of the black feathers, seeming to grasp something. You remember where you wanted to go.

You leave iAPM. The red electronic billboards in the night sky flash. Inexplicably your line of sight is drawn to them – there's a reason they were designed red. The frequency of their flickering seems to synchronise with the sound of the surrounding environment. You can hear it. The sound is broadcast at regular intervals: the wind passing through holes in the office building's wall; the water evaporating from the plane tree leaves; the water from the ruptured pipe flooding the ground; and the homeless children crying – the white noise of an electric current from nowhere... They fall on their respective beats, working seamlessly, in tandem, to shape tuneless music; it makes your blood run cold.

It makes you fall deeply into it, without resistance, in a second or maybe in ten thousand years, you can't even tell anymore.

You want to escape, you have seen the crowds. Or something that you think looks like crowds.

On the roads, people (or maybe they're not people) have made it through Xiangyang Park, everyone seems to be wearing the wrong clothes, they're walking gawkily towards you. These were once retired old aunties, takeaway delivery boys, gym members, middle-aged traffic managers, mixed-race twins, white-collar office women: they were humanoid creatures. But now synchronised smiles are on their faces, smiles which seem to come from Alpha Centauri, 4.22 light years away, full of invincible escapist charm. They stretch their hands out to you, not in unison, but more terribly than that. It's more like they are the organs of an enormous and transparent body, with the retired auntie passing a nerve impulse to the takeaway boy, and then at some distance affecting the female office worker and the mixed-race twins, with every person intertwining, expanding from the person preceding them, as in Giacomo Balla's futurist works, like a peacock's tail fanning and dancing in the night, its doubling shadows generating persistence of vision.

Flustered, you evade their brandished tentacles. In the cracks and fissures of their bodies, you seem to travel through the 180 years since Shanghai became a treaty port, going from its old Western-style garden houses to the new towers with chic faces and old-fashioned slogans, rapidly revolving, collaging, colliding, assimilating to a single whole.

You understand that what they're doing now is inviting you in. But you don't want to be integrated.

You still have a way to hurry, on this last day of the Anthropocene.

Something is absorbing your consciousness, like a bag of activated carbon in the fridge, absorbing it through minuscule but invisible holes, the remnants of your self are weakening, are being compressed into slender spaghetti noodles, trembling and swaying in the neon lights, flowing into some transparent body that administers everyone in the park, perhaps everyone in the whole city. It does not want to let you go.

You feel weak and terrified, like some flying insect caught in a spiderweb, trying to beat slender, membrane-like wings, but only tearing open greater wounds, as everything you ever cherished is being pulverised out of this wound.

A whirlpool begins to swirl in your mouth. Those flavours anchored to particular moments in your life float one by one off your tongue and vanish: the blood-rust taste from a tumble on the cinder track; the turbid green seawater forced down your trachea; the sticky perspiration behind the ear one summer afternoon; the messy first kiss; the brown medicinal tea distilling the essence from numberless animal corpses; the braised beef shank right out of the wok – the small differences between all those gradually fade, finally blending into a similar flavour, a metallic astringency, and then even that taste vanishes.

The world trembles even harder, like light trying to break free from a black hole, and you know it's futile.

Something is pressed into your hand. Something small. Like a button.

'Swallow it,' a voice says.

You do, and the world calms down, those noodles have been cut.

20mg of Jonno, works out at ten times a dose of Ritalin; it can get you through an hour, maybe.

You nod your head like you understood what the words mean. You finally grasp where the voice comes from; it comes from an oversized black hoodie enveloping a petite body. You confront one another without moving a muscle.

The shadows of the hoodie disclose a face. You see that you're of the same kind, but a different sex, to judge by the features not fully adult.

'So where are you going?'

You think about how to answer.

'These drugs saved my ass. For exams I used to take them every day, for about two months.' There doesn't seem to be any need to respond, though the voice continues, urgent. 'Maybe they screwed me up, who knows.'

The face distorts, revealing some kind of expression, but you've lost the ability to interpret it. Your thoughts are still dwelling on that word, exams. You should be able to draw more information from that word, but you can't.

'Can I see?'

It takes a good while before you understood that your interlocutor is talking about the book in your hand, so you pass it over, saying, 'I'm going to return it.'

'Return? To whom?' Black Hoodie flips to the library stamp and the spine label. 'Oh, Shanghai Library, I used to revise there all the time.'

Revise. There's a word to make you sink deep into thought.

'Why do you want to return it? Everything's ending, cognition has collapsed, all the plans to restart the mind have failed, or maybe that's what triggered it all, you know the story, oh, or maybe you don't.'

You're silent for a long time, and in the open-concept fitness club across the road, naked men and women machines are working out. You can't tell whether it's real or an illusion.

Six roads lead from this intersection, and the traffic lights go from red to green as regulated. Although there is nothing to prevent you from proceeding, the lights still seem to bear on your behaviour, just like returning the book, an internalised heritage of civilisation, like a Skinner box.[2] Resistance and obedience are two sides of the mirror – you require this kind of illusion.

I get it, everybody has things they want to do, every eggshell breaks into different shapes. Like them: what they've decided is to give themselves to a greater consciousness. Black Hoodie points to the crowds in the park, now they're chasing a stray dog. 'Maybe after tonight they'll represent the new direction.'

You shake your head, you seem a little lost, it seems like the button's effect might be wearing off. You carefully look at every road. You had thought you'd be able to remember them, but you should have marked the roads on your body. You're a bit frustrated.

Just keep walking down that road.

It seems like Black Hoodie can see your thoughts – that's an amazing skill, perhaps after today this person will become a spirit of the new world, as long as there are enough buttons, as long as the buttons keep working.

'Maybe you're the last person I can talk to.' The black hoodie shrugs its shoulders, distorting its face in another way. 'Don't look at me that way, I'm not going with you, I have my own stuff to take care of. I don't know how long I can stay conscious, before I run out of drugs, I have to get stuff done.'

You see that tree, it catches the eye, though you've actually always ignored its existence. The crotch of the tree is covered with hanging bits of paper with colour pictures on them, if you look carefully it's like every one of the pictures wants to suck you into it, wants to shrink you down to a tiny size, and from the lines and patches of colours, numberless details emerge, like an omnipresent and self-contained world. You can look at it without interruption, and seem to find an angle from which to pass through the various papers. So all the papers become windows, and the world is interconnected.

'Wa.' You utter a syllable, because you really don't know how to describe the feeling.

'Yeah, I know,' Black Hoodie nods, seemingly satisfied with your response. 'Sometimes I feel like they existed long before the advent of humanity, like they're just borrowing my hand to paint with. Maybe after humans, there will still be someone else, I don't know, like spirits? Who can understand it all. They'll live longer than me.'

You nod too, and the beautiful bits of paper almost make you forget your original destination. You force yourself to leave the tree, leave the black hoodie, and cross the street against the red light.

The city will survive. Maybe artificial intelligence will be more intelligent without the involvement of humanity. Algorithms require time to develop variation, to evolve patterns over trillions of generations that are compatible with nature. Maybe the Earth has chosen to reboot, at the cost of shutting down some redundant apps.

You skirt the heaps of destroyed cars that litter Huaihai Road, as well as the pink bubbling slime covering the road surface, and the crowds of people all kneeling to lick it, like herds of animals gathering around water on the savannah.

A sweet-looking girl is mimicking the GPS navigation: 'Turn right up ahead and then turn right up ahead.' She is repeating the route, her feet seemingly not moving at all.

Through the buildings you can almost see the Yan'an Elevated Road, now ablaze – a long fuse lacerating the night. You just think it's very beautiful.

The button has lost its effect entirely. You feel like you are floating three feet above your own body, and it's as if any gust of wind might blow your spirit and your flesh in different directions. The only thing you can do is to strain to remember the memories bound up in the flesh, for happiness is always superficial, while the fetters of pain are the deepest, firmest.

You wander through this museum of pain, with the figure of a woman, like a wandering spirit, projected on every exhibition piece you walk past, like an overzealous tour guide. You stand at the end of the corridor, at the tightly closed scarlet doors, and the woman floats inside while you are shut out. You lift your hand to caress the perfectly smooth surface of the door, but your palm gets trapped in it, warm and sticky, with unsettling contractions and tremors. You yank your hand out again, and the blood comes welling out of the door, gushing across your body.

Now you finally understand who the woman is.

At a certain moment you see the Shanghai streets of a million years from now, the tilting towers ensnared in gigantic, serpentine reeds, the seawater brushing gently over your pubis and on the seafloor surge countless tiny shadows like cars on a highway – you grasp clearly that these are not fish.

You are still standing on the street, you realise, but the world has become even more strange. You faintly recall that you want to move forward, that white building, like a temple of public worship, is just across the street from you.

You don't know if it's just a step away or at the other end of the world.

Maybe it's the same thing.

The famous statue next to you opens its mouth and begins to speak. It says:

The game is extremely overheated, and there isn't any mystery, any religion, nor transported people, even who willingly become one another, it's a part of the world that has been passed through, enough to change the aesthetics congealing in individual viruses.*

'What?' you ask.

It starts to sing:

Experiencing the limitless is almost amazing. Of course, even yourself ought to be a regret. It is all for the honour of the totally suspenceless visit, You feel nightmares, without her what is the self, it is only wanting why. But this begins with the turn of real mathematical power, it is very hard to lose the afterwards, to change the future's website, as well as assisting the surface of ceremony, pretending that it is somewhere concealed, but can only face the crowds.

An authentic tumour.*

You stop trying to understand, you give up your questioning. If this is how your consciousness maps onto an objective world on the cusp of disintegration, then it's only to be expected for everything to initiate dialogue with you. Profoundly meaningful, brilliantly insightful, totally incomprehensible dialogues. And in fact, not every object will open its mouth. You try to discover the rules, but you don't have the ability. Perhaps you once wanted to save the world, but now all that's left is sorrow.

Before long there won't even be sorrow anymore.

Step by step you approach the end, the reverberations of the world distract you. They come from the fallen leaves, the trash cans, the bird shit on the steps, the graffiti on the electricity poles, the dazzle of the traffic lights, the irregularities of the skyline, of the cloudscape. Not only do they speak, they have expressions too, and they seem more expressive than the contortions on a human face. You can't explain it, you're just surrounded by the vortex of all the objects' emotions.

Liquid begins to well uncontrollably out of your eyes. The world trembles, blurs. A carefully rehearsed grand performance accompanies your every action and touch, like interlocking gears, seamless. They sing solos, call-and-response songs, then *tutti*:

The raging wind fills with the naked fringe, he hides the room in the sporting consciousness.

Blackout for the cartoon, constructing a whole life, the membrane pulls open concentration.

You reveal your black eyes, your pale skin fills the bed like deep sleep, hundreds of lightning bolts, again slowly initiating a bout of nausea.

Time goes forward and reverses so that the trance is dispelled, stuck before us is the starry sky. But I don't see my own completely crazy land, entering the new world is such a free motion, or to put it more precisely is OK.

You raise your head again, putting those illusions emerging incompletely. But he has left you, disappeared in the morning glow. Surrounded like satin.*

Amid the music's strains, you ascend the stairs like a monarch, the book in your hand expanding and contracting, panting heavily.

The automatic door does not automatically revolve, nor does it reflect you. As you walk over shards of glass into the shrine of knowledge, it's like a typhoon has passed through, the wet pages of books plastered wherever the eye wanders. It's as though someone has been sorting through the heritage of human knowledge in this cavernous space, five storeys high. The white ceiling-light flickers, and you stand there, waiting for someone to materialise, to point to the labyrinth's exit. All these printed words no longer carry any meaning for you.

A long shriek escapes you, the sound clattering along the spiral staircase, then weakening to a metallic hum.

You clearly make out the click of the timer reaching zero, so booming in the deathly silence.

Some time later, you hear an echo from the Foreign Journals Reading Room, the Famous Authors Manuscript Archive, from the Document Restoration Exhibition Hall and the Braille Reading Room – a sticky, brittle, unhuman echo.

That exquisite white machine in front of you emits a tender, alluring light. Its slot, enveloped in silver metal, is so smooth and compact that it seems that the book in your hands need only to be inserted for you to forget all the metaphysical irritations of the world. It awaits you. This is the role ordained for you since the birth of the universe.

Your face is expressionless, pretending that thought has led you to make this decision.

The book soundlessly slides from your hands to the floor, like a skein of wrinkled skin.

You walk out of the machine, and into the dark night, into the ancient, into the new world.

Into me.

Notes

* The passages marked with an asterisk were generated by AI programmes trained on deep learning of the author's style, and have not thereafter been subject to human editing.

1. iAPM is a luxury brand mall in central Shanghai. For a Moncler campaign in 2017, Liu Bolin, photographed by Annie Leibowitz, was pictured in one of his well-known 'camouflage' installations, in this case 'disappearing' into an iceberg by means of clothing and make-up.

2. Also known as an Operant Conditioning Chamber; a laboratory apparatus used to study animal behaviour (most often rats or mice), created by B. F. Skinner while he was a graduate student at Harvard University.

About the Authors

Wang Anyi (born 1954) is a novelist, screenwriter, and short story writer. She is the author of over 100 short stories, 40 novelettes, 10 novels, and various essays and prose pieces. Her most famous work is *The Song of Everlasting Sorrow*, which was adapted for screen (by Stanley Kwan), television (by Ding Hei) and stage. She is among the most widely read authors of the post-Mao era and is one of China's most influential and innovative writers. She has won numerous awards including the Mao Dun Literature Award in 2000, and her novel *Baotown* has been nominated for the *Los Angeles Times'* Book of the Year, and the 2011 Man Booker International Prize. She lives in Shanghai and is currently chair of the Writers' Association of Shanghai, and professor of Chinese literature and creative writing at Fudan University.

Xiao Bai was born in 1968 in Shanghai. He is the author of *Horny Hamlet*, a prize-winning collection of essays, and the novel *Game Point*. In 2013 his novella, *Xu Xiangbi the Spy*, won the tenth annual Shanghai Literary Prize, and in 2018 his novella *Blockade* won the Lu Xun Literary Prize. *French Concession* (HarperCollins, 2015) was his first novel to be translated into English. He lives in Shanghai.

Chen Danyan was born in 1958 in Beijing, and moved to Shanghai as a child. After studying Chinese literature at East China Normal University (1978–1982), she worked as an editor for the Children's *Epoch* magazine. Her autobiographical novel *Nine Lives* (1992) dealt with childhood experiences of the Cultural Revolution, and received the UNESCO Prize for Peace and Tolerance and was nominated for the 1996 German Youth Literature Prize. She is best known for her trilogy of biographical narratives: *Shanghai Memorabilia, Shanghai Princess,* and *Shanghai Beauty,* and central to her recent work is an exploration of the lives of younger generations (in particular young women), growing up in the context of China's one-child policy.

Shen Dacheng is a columnist, novelist, short story writer and editor. After graduating from Shanghai University in Industrial Management, she worked in marketing and then began a column (featuring short stories based on real characters' lives) called 'Strange People' in the literary publication *Sprout*. Real name Xu Xiaoqian, she takes her pen name from a popular Shanghai pastry shop. Her first collection *The Ones in Remembrance* was published in 2017. Her 2018 short story 'Miss Box Man' is set in a world of virus-induced fear, where the rich live in sealed containers which protect them from the pathogen, and the rest live a life of a constant, compulsory blood tests and hosings-down with disinfectant. She is currently working on a new collection to be titled *Asteroids in the Afternoon.*

Cai Jun is one of China's bestselling horror writers. He started his writing career at twenty-two and was quickly awarded the Bertelsmann People's Literature Award for New Writers. His novels include *The Tower of Black Swan, Mysterious Message, Murdering Things Past,* and the serialised novel *The*

Longest Night. His novel *19th Floor of Hell* won the Sina Literary Award and is one of three of Jun's novels to have been made into a feature film. Two of his books have been developed into television series, and his work has been translated into six languages.

Chen Qiufan (born 1981), also known as **Stanley Chan**, is a science fiction writer, columnist, and scriptwriter. His first novel *The Waste Tide*, (originally published in 2013) has been translated into English by Ken Liu and published by Tor & Head of Zeus in 2019. His short stories have won three Galaxy Awards for Chinese Science Fiction, and twelve Nebula Awards for Science Fiction and Fantasy in Chinese. 'The Fish of Lijiang' received the Best Short Form Award for the 2012 Science Fiction & Fantasy Translation Awards. His stories have been published in *Fantasy & Science Fiction, MIT Technology Review, Clarkesworld, Year's Best SF, Interzone*, and *Lightspeed*, as well as influential Chinese science fiction magazine *Science Fiction World*.

Xia Shang (born in Shanghai, 1969) is a novelist, often associated with the post-avant-garde school of Chinese writers, as well as a graphic designer. He is the author of the novels *East Coast Chronicle, The Lazarus Child's Wandering, Taxidermist* and *Bare Undead*. He currently lives between Shanghai and New York.

Teng Xiaolan was born in Shanghai in 1976, and began writing in 2001. Her first short story collection, *Ten Roses*, was published in 2005. She has had pieces featured in *People's Literature* magazine and various other literary journals. She received the Lu Xun Literature Prize for her novella *A Beautiful Day*.

Fu Yuehui was born in Baoshan, Yunnan Province in 1984. He was among the first class to graduate from Fudan University's Literary Writing MFA, and has had short stories printed in a number of publications including *Mountain Flowers*, *Shanghai Wenxue*, *Master*, *Chinese Writers*, *Youth Literature*, *Changcheng*, *Hongdou* and *Dianchi*. In 2009, he received the Emerging Short Story Author Award from *Shanghai Wenxue*.

Wang Zhanhei is one of China's most successful young writers, and author of two short story collections, *Air Cannon,* which won the inaugural Blancpain-Imaginist Literary Prize, and *Neighborhood Adventurers*, which focuses on the lives of working class urban Chinese people. Her work often focuses on the Shanghai neighbourhood of Dinghai Bridge. A graduate from Fudan University, she also works as a high-school teacher.

About the Translators

Lee Anderson studied Chinese at the University of Leeds, where he then went on to gain an MA in translation. Now based in London, he has spent the past ten years working as a medical and technical translator from both Chinese and French. This is his first published literary translation.

Yu Yan Chen is an award-winning poet and literary translator. She won Singapore's Golden Point Award in 2015 and garnered the top prize at the Flushing Poetry Festival in 2019. Her first poetry collection, entitled *Small Hours*, was published by NYQ Books in 2011. Her second collection, *Grandma Says*, was published in 2017. She has translated short stories, essays and poems by Yi Sha, Mai Jia, Li Juan, Han Dong and Zheng Xiaoqiong.

Jack Hargreaves is a Chinese-English translator from East Yorkshire, now based in London. Specialising in literary and academic translation, his work has appeared on *Asymptote Journal*, *Paper Republic* and *LA Review of Books China Channel* and includes writing by Zhu Yiye, Isaac Hsu, Yuan Ling and Ye Duoduo. Forthcoming translations include Li Juan's *Winter Pasture*, Yang Dian's flash fiction collection *A Contrarian's Tales* and *A History of Chinese Philosophical Thought* by Zhang Xianghao.

Paul Harris studied Chinese at Oxford in the 1960s, then followed a 35-year career, mostly as a translator in the financial sector. Following retirement, for 13 years he went to China regularly on two-monthly assignments as a volunteer English teacher. He has more recently developed an interest in literary translation. Another of his short-story translations (of 'Where Did I Lose You?' by Fan Xiaoqing) appears on the website Paper Republic – Chinese Literature in Translation.

Frances Nichols is a Chinese to English translator currently living in Madrid. Frances lived and worked in Chengdu, China for six years before running a translation company in London and going solo in 2016.

Christopher MacDonald is a translator and public service interpreter based in South Wales. He previously lived and worked for over twenty years in Taiwan and the PRC. He has an MA in Translation & Interpretation and an MSc in Sustainability & Adaptation Planning, and is a Member of the Chartered Institute of Linguists. His published work includes *The Science of War: Sun Tzu's Art of War* re-translated and re-considered (2018). In 2019 he won the Comma Press Emerging Translator Award.

Carson Ramsdell is a Beijing-based translator from the United States currently studying a master's degree in Chinese Philosophy at Renmin University. His research focuses on how Chinese history and philosophy shape lived experience in modern China. Through translation he hopes to use transmissions of the everyday to break down the cultural-linguistic barriers between China and the world.

Josh Stenberg is a Senior Lecturer in Chinese Studies at the University of Sydney. He is the author of *Minority Stages: Sino-*

Indonesian Performance and Public Display (University of Hawaii Press, 2019) and the translator/editor of four books of contemporary Chinese fiction.

Katherine Tse received her BA in English from UCLA and MA in Translation from the University of Leeds. She started translating during her six years in Taipei and has since worked for clients across Asia and Europe. She was named the Rising Star of 2019 by the Globalization and Localization Association. After living in Shanghai and Leeds (UK), Katherine is now based in the southern US. Find her at tsetranslation.com.

Helen Wang is a curator at the British Museum, and an award-winning translator both in the UK (Marsh Award 2017) and China (Chen Bochui Award 2017). She works with Paper Republic, the Leeds Centre for New Chinese Writing, and Chinese Books for Young Readers.

ALSO AVAILABLE IN THIS SERIES

The Book of Cairo

Edited by Raph Cormack

'Ten compelling new voices' – *Bookmunch*

Once the centre of the ancient world and, for a thousand years, a welcoming destination for explorers and tourists, Cairo has more recently become a city determined to forget. Since 2013, the events of Tahrir Square and Rabaa al-Adawiya have been gradually erased from its official history; writers have been imprisoned, publishing houses raided, and independent news sites shut down by the authorities. With the Egyptian government currently moving many of its ministries to the desert new builds, east of Cairo, the city's future (as well as its past) seem uncertain.

Here ten new voices offer tentative glimpses into the city's life at a time when writing directly about its greatest challenges is often too dangerous. With satire, surrealism, humour and a flair for the microcosm, these stories guide us through the slums and suburbs, bars and backstreets of a city haunted by an unspoken past.

Featuring: Featuring Hassan Abdel Mawgoud, Eman Abdelrahim, Nael Eltoukhy, Areej Gamal, Hatem Hafez, Hend Ja'far, Nahla Karam, Mohamed Kheir, Ahmed Naji & Mohamed Salah al-Azab

ISBN: 978-1-91097-425-4
£9.99

The Book of Tehran

Edited by Fereshteh Ahmadi

'A beautiful, insightful peek into a lesser-explored
area of the world and its literature.' – *Storgy*

A city of stories – short, fragmented, amorphous, and at times
contradictory – Tehran is an impossible tale to tell. For the capital
city of one of the most powerful nations in the Middle East, its
literary output is rarely acknowledged in the West. This unique
celebration of its writing brings together ten stories exploring the
tensions and pressures that make the city what it is: tensions between
the public and the private, pressures from without – judgemental
neighbours, the expectations of religion and society – and from
within – family feuds, thwarted ambitions, destructive relationships.
The psychological impact of these pressures manifests in different
ways: a man wakes up to find a stranger relaxing in his living room
and starts to wonder if this is his house at all; a struggling writer
decides only when his girlfriend breaks his heart will his work have
depth... In all cases, coping with these pressures leads us, the readers,
into an unexpected trove of cultural treasures – like the burglar, in
one story, descending into the basement of a mysterious antique
collector's house – treasures of which we, in the West, are almost
wholly ignorant.

*Featuring: Fereshteh Ahmadi, Atoosa Afshin-Navid, Kourosh Asadi,
Azardokht Bahrami, Hamed Habibi, Mohammad Hosseini, Amirhossein
Khorshidfar, Payam Nasser, Goli Taraghi & Mohammad Tolouei*

ISBN: 978-1-91097-424-7
£9.99

The Book of Khartoum

Edited by Raph Cormack & Max Shmookler

'An exciting, long-awaited collection showcasing
some of Sudan's finest writers.' – *Leila Aboulela*

Khartoum, according to one theory, takes its name from the Beja
word *hartooma*, meaning 'meeting place'. Geographically, culturally
and historically, the Sudanese capital is certainly that: a meeting place
of the Blue and White Niles, a confluence of Arabic and African
histories, and a destination point for countless refugees displaced by
Sudan's long, troubled history of forced migration.

In the pages of this book, the city also stands as a meeting place for
ideas: where the promise and glamour of the big city meets its tough
social realities; where traces of a colonial past are still visible in day-
to-day life; where the dreams of a young boy, playing in his father's
shop, act out a future that may one day be his. Diverse literary styles
also come together here: the political satire of Ahmed al-Malik; the
surrealist poetics of Bushra al-Fadil; the social realism of the first
postcolonial authors; and the lyrical abstraction of the new 'Iksir'
generation. As with any great city, it is from these complex tensions
that the best stories begin.

*Featuring: Bushra al-Fadil, Isa al-Hilu, Ali al-Makk, Ahmed al-Malik,
Bawadir Bashir, Mamoun Eltlib, Rania Mamoun, Abdel Aziz Baraka
Sakin, Arthur Gabriel Yak & Hammour Ziada.*

ISBN: 978-1-90558-372-0
£9.99

Points of Origin

Diao Dou

'Diao Dou's stories brim with surreal and caustic humor.'
– *Hari Kunzru*

A letter-writing campaign goes awry when a law is passed that only allows people to walk the streets at night, if they maintain a squatting position at all times...

A town is overrun with cockroaches; despite the government's official expressions of concern, the only person doing anything about it is branded an agitator...

A widower is forced to move into the city to live with his son, bringing his cat and his strange country ways with him...

Diao Dou's short stories perform a kind of high-wire literary acrobatics; each one executes an immaculate mid-air transition, from closely observed social realism to surrealist parody, and back again. Covering all aspects of modern Chinese life – from the high-minded morals of an emerging middle class, to the vividly remembered hardships of an all-too-recent collectivist past – these stories offer a very particular window into the contemporary Chinese psyche, and show a culture struggling to keep pace with the extraordinary transformations that have befallen it in the space of a single lifetime.

Diao Dou is wildly regarded as one of China's leading satirists, praised for his refusal to follow any of the numerous literary trends that often dominate the Chinese literary scene.

ISBN: 978-1-90558-362-1
£9.99